ACCLAIM FOR
WIDOWS IN THE DARK

"Answers the urgent financial questions distressed and grieving women ask themselves."

—Margaret Gault, Certified Financial Planner

"Mrs. Gatov's book has been an essential tool in helping me learn how to handle my finances with self-confidence. Through fact-filled chapters with helpful illustrative material, it guides one easily through the intricacies of money management."

**—Malca Chall, recent widow,
Interviewer-Editor, Bancroft Library,
University of California**

"I know from experience that too many married women are underinformed about the management of personal finances. When they become widows they are frightened by their ignorance. *Widows in the Dark* treats this matter with understanding and explains clearly the difference between the various sorts of investments, and the language used about them by professionals in the field and the financial journals."

**—Gregg Elberg, President,
First Federal Savings and
Loan Association, San Rafael**

"Warm and helpful . . . levelheaded . . . you feel you have a personal friend in Elizabeth Gatov. You will want to keep this close by for reference. Be careful about lending it."

—Raleigh News and Observer

ELIZABETH SMITH GATOV had been deeply involved in California politics before President John F. Kennedy appointed her Treasurer of the United States. She was the first woman invited into his administration. She has been a feature editor, a lobbyist, a vigorous lecturer on American government, and has always been very active in community and civic affairs. An important figure in the Democratic Party and well respected for her political acumen, she is considered to have made an indelible mark on California and national politics.

WIDOWS IN THE DARK

Rescuing Your Financial Position

Elizabeth Smith Gatov
Former Treasurer of the United States

A Warner Communications Company

WARNER BOOKS EDITION

Originally published by Common Knowledge Press, a division of Commonweal, a nonprofit center for service and research in health and human ecology, P.O. Box 316, Bolinas, CA 94924.

Cover photo by Dan Wagner

Warner Books, Inc.
666 Fifth Avenue
New York, N.Y. 10103

A Warner Communications Company

Printed in the United States of America

First Warner Books Printing: April, 1986

10 9 8 7 6 5 4 3 2 1

To my late husband, Albert W. Gatov, with whom my twenty-year relationship was passed in so much laughter and warmth, I was scarcely aware of anything so fundamental as the management of money. He never believed how ignorant I was about it, and I did little to let him know. Toward the end, he assured me everything would be all right, and it was. But not exactly the way he imagined.

Contents

MAYOR DIANNE FEINSTEIN

Foreword

When Elizabeth Gatov's beloved husband, Al, died, she found herself in a situation familiar to many widows. She had to take on the burdens of financial management that had always been her husband's responsibility—and she had to do it at a time of enormous emotional stress.

Libby—who is never called anything but that—is a woman of tremendous capabilities who served as one of this nation's outstanding Treasurers of the United States. She has superb qualifications and talent galore.

Having been through the trials and trauma of widowhood myself, I know that there are many women without Elizabeth's great gift of readily understanding the murky world of finance. Looking back at that difficult time in my own life, I can say that I wish I had had access to a book as simple and comprehensible as the pages you are about to read.

Widows in the Dark explains simply and compassionately the many choices that any widow faced with the management of assets, small or large, needs to understand. It translates the jargon of the money world into plain English. The book is also deeply sensitive to human needs—and the author's comments on her personal experiences of widowhood are as insightful and invaluable as her financial advice.

I am delighted to recommend *Widows in the Dark* not only to those who must face or are experiencing widowhood, but also to any woman—young or old—who has left her financial affairs in the hands of someone else. We all have a compelling need to know more about finance in today's world, and Elizabeth Gatov's book provides a splendid guide to improved understanding of this vital area.

Acknowledgments

For their encouragement and help in many different ways, I can finally thank publicly:
Nancy Blanchet, Kim Schoknecht, Bruce McGregor, Martin Huff, Michael Lerner, Dr. William Lamers, Wendy Foster Evans, James D. White, L. Jay Stewart, Michael Larsen, William Matson Roth, Joan and Don Collins, Nancy and Howard Jewel, Nancy Swadesh, Malca Chall, David Nelson, Alan Cranston, Dianne Feinstein, Gregg Elberg, Margaret Gault, Florence Sinton, Kit Cole, Eleanor Cranston Cameron, Adele Horowitz, Janice Ury, Cyr Copertini, Kay Moore, Olga Baxt, Carol Peckham, Nancy Westberg and my stepdaughter Barbara Gatov and my son Daniel Upham Smith. Between them, the last two taught me the basics of filing and record keeping, and got me started.

Grateful acknowledgment is also made for permission to reprint the following material in this book:

"Money Market Mutual Funds" chart. Copyright © 1984 by The New York Times Company and the Tribune Media Service. Reprinted by permission.

Introduction

When Irving Berlin wrote his great song "Together," he must have had two people like us in mind. When I married Al Gatov, we had already reached an age in life that was relatively comfortable. We each had previous spouses and children with same. Our respective children were making their own ways and we relished thoughts of a new journey in life that matched our hopes. We lived in Marin county, California, close enough to San Francisco to maintain a pulse on our shared political interests. We swam happily in the mainstream of our state and the community as well.

Fun, love, and laughter filled our years together. We often agreed we should spend some time examining and discussing our financial matters, and promised ourselves we would. Unfortunately, procrastination took possession of our wits and we never did it. One day, all too soon, cancer claimed the life of Al Gatov.

Suddenly I was reduced to a state of shock and utter helplessness. Nothing made sense. Distraught, beside myself, I wandered aimlessly around the house struggling to accept the fact that he was gone and wondering how I would cope. It became clear that I must come to grips with our investments, but reading or talking about them might as well have been in a foreign language. It was a financially oriented jargon with which I was totally unfamiliar. I soon learned that my plight was not unlike that of thousands of women who find themselves in similar situations. Quickly I came to know the meaning of the word "widow" and I began to seek help. More than most widows, I might have been expected to know about money. I was Treasurer of the United States in the John F. Kennedy Administration (Elizabeth Rudel Smith), and for fifteen years before that I was a director of my family's machine tool company. Since 1963, I have been a vice-president and director of a savings and loan association in California.

All these experiences taught me how to understand financial statements and something about economics but not a thing about personal money management. I was ignorant and, worse, self-conscious about my ignorance when dealing with professionals in the field.

Records indicate fourteen million or so widows in this country have suddenly found themselves responsible for their own financial future at a stage in life when learning new skills is hard, especially when we don't know where to turn for the knowledge we need.

This book offers simple, direct information and reassuring counsel that comes from firsthand experience and an understanding of the emotional and economic distress a woman in this position feels. I found the road to peace of mind and a sense of security gained by learning the basics of personal money management.

Using this book, you will learn how to:

- Read and understand the financial pages of your newspaper
- Choose professionals wisely to help you manage your investments
- Understand the execution of your husband's will
- Anticipate where your money comes from, when, and in what amounts

- Maintain good financial records and enjoy the process
- Plan for tax, mortgage, insurance, and other fixed payments
- Create your own net worth statement
- Achieve a rewarding sense of financial independence through a grasp of the fundamentals of investing
- Make sound financial decisions with confidence

This book could not have been written without the generous help of Nancy Blanchet, stockbroker, Kim Schoknecht, attorney, Bruce McGregor, investment counselor, and Martin Huff, management consultant, who all helped lead me through the maze of legal and financial jargon of trust and probate, stocks and bonds, and investments to the point where I can have an intelligent conversation about them without fear of embarrassment.

If you are at the same stage of nearly zero comprehension of these matters, as were all save one of the forty-seven widows who so kindly shared their experiences with me, I hope you will gain an informational base from this book that will help you to relax in the comfort of knowledge.

Elizabeth Smith Gatov, 1985
Kentfield, California

CHAPTER ONE

The Scene

Married to a financially competent man whose income was enough during our marriage so that meeting our obligations was no special problem, our life seemed very stable. The marriage worked well; we both enjoyed it. That happiness made it more difficult to accept life now.

I knew that Al made investments from time to time because he would mention them occasionally. He had a pension and carried life insurance, although I never knew how much. His major financial concern always seemed to be taxes. Like most men, he grumbled about them constantly, but there was always enough money for everything we needed or wanted to do. Always bothered by the uncertainties of the economy and interest rates, he felt he was working rather well with the situation utilizing a tax shelter the Internal Revenue Service had yet to disallow. He spoke of moving money around to cushion the vagaries of the business climate, but I understood nothing about that. I only knew our lives were in good order.

When the last child went off to college and the rest were in pursuit of their own careers, we traveled a lot and enjoyed a sense of privacy we had almost forgotten existed. Heretofore, the family always came first and fulfilling this task was a role we both played. As head of the household, Al was making the major decisions about his career—where we lived, what automobiles were purchased, and lots of other things I left to him and/or ignored. On reflection, he seldom mentioned specific financial concerns that might have worried him; only his major or minor triumphs called for a day's end report.

My husband planned his investments with knowledge acquired over the years from formal and informal conversations, reading, and consultations with professionals. As a result of this long and tested experience, he knew how to work with specialists in law, investments, taxes, and insurance. He knew enough about how business in general operated to feel confident. However, we did not share in building this backlog of experience because I was developing my own expertise in different areas.

Death is a fact no one likes to confront, so the subject is seldom discussed. Life is the more immediate thing, and life seemed more harmonious and exhilarating than I ever thought possible. Free of responsibilities, except for each other of course, we assumed that it would go on like this indefinitely. Our situation seemed so secure financially and emotionally.

We casually and almost automatically evolved an informal division of labor when I started running the household affairs years ago and managed efficiently the household accounts. He made the larger financial decisions with equal competence.

Division of labor or responsibility quickly becomes a matter of habit. A stockbroker made the following comments about what he found was the "woman's role" in the family investment program. "Sometimes I telephone and the wife answers. When I tell her who I am, she almost always says, 'Oh, you'll have to talk to my husband—I don't know anything about this.' Or, 'You'll want to speak to my husband.'

"When I see the husband next, I ask him why he doesn't explain his investments to his wife, or I suggest that she might like to come in and see me about them. Usually, he just shrugs and says she isn't interested." The broker said at that point he feels he's at the end of his rope and has gone as far as he can take the matter.

All too experienced at trying to deal with distraught widows who are totally ignorant about investments, he expressed himself rather tartly: "I don't think women are nearly assertive enough about these matters. It's just a cop-out. Preserving their money should be equally important to both of them, especially with their different life expectancies. She was his partner in accumulating a certain amount of wealth, but then she steps aside as though money were something dirty that she doesn't care to be involved with."

Asked if he didn't find that some men *want* their wives to stay out of the family investment decision, he replied he had rarely found that to be true. He said he couldn't understand why any woman would want to remain ignorant about the family's resources, especially if she understood that their investments might someday be her major source of support.

In your case, it might have seemed that money management was something you didn't *need* to know since you relied on your husband's judgment, which served you both well. Or perhaps you felt—in spite of what this stockbroker said—that a lot of men regard questions about something they are in charge of as a question of their ability to *be* in charge of it. Some time in the late 1970s you might have inquired about your General Motors stock, mentioning that you were seeing more and more small foreign cars on the road. An innocent query like this raised at breakfast could have been interpreted, if your husband felt threatened, as an oblique criticism of his financial judgment that might have spoiled the day and dinner too. Since you spoke of seeing so many foreign cars, he might have concluded that you thought he had made a mistake in holding onto the General Motors stock. This is not idle speculation. Any sensitive wife does not need to poke a nerve more than once. She may not understand just what it is about a certain subject that upsets her husband; the fact that something does is usually reason enough to leave it alone, especially if it is not important to her in the first place.

As an example of this situation, a recent spate of magazine articles describes wives who have upset their husbands by venturing into fields they had never thought of, or at least not mentioned, before. "My Wife is Forty-Five and She Wants a Job!" or "I'm Putting My Middle-Aged Wife Through Law School!" At least one widower took the law school article seriously. After many years alone, he was about to marry a bride fifteen years younger than himself, so he took care of his worries by putting a clause in their marriage contract that she would never go to law school. She signed it and is quite content to continue remodeling houses, which she had successfully done for some time. Perhaps something is unsettling to a businessman about having a lawyer in his bed. Or he may have been disinclined to compete for her time against her law career. In any event, an experienced wife can sense what constitutes a threat to her husband and what does not.

Many (perhaps most) women have no idea how much money would be available to them if their husband died. Often, one just signs the joint income tax return dutifully and without questions. A casual glance at income tax forms reveals very little indeed, and unless you spend several hours studying the figures, it is murky information. Though married for years, I was certainly no equal partner in managing the family's financial resources—or "assets" in legalese. Trapped in the conspiracy of silence and disinterest that ensnarls so many married women in the higher tax brackets, it is a cultural habit and also a cultural deprivation.

You are a bit like the well-born Chinese woman of generations back whose feet were bound when she was a little girl to keep them small, fitting in tiny shoes. That her feet had been painfully deformed was unimportant because it was assumed she would never need them to walk on anyway. As an aristocrat, she would be carried wherever she went.

Husbands seldom worry about how you will manage alone. Al knew that his lawyer would take charge of the will, his broker or investment counselor would know all about the family investments, and the tax accountant, who had been guiding him for years, would prepare the tax returns. His insurance agent would send the necessary forms to fill out and promptly pay off the claims on his life insurance policies. Then his company would take care of my pensions rights. He confidently believed I would be all set, but he was wrong. Missing was the most basic kind of information. Who were these people? Unless your husband was noteworthy so that his death was given prominence in the press, none of these people he relied upon to help may have known of it. As one woman put it, "Whenever I brought up the matter of his will, he just assured me that I would be well cared for. But the trouble was, he had just drawn up a new will, and I didn't even know the lawyer's name!"

It would be fairly normal for you not to know the names of the people your husband had consulted for professional advice. He dealt with them over his office phone or at lunch, and you may not have ever met them. You might also have felt hesitant about broaching a subject such as money management, which you knew nothing about yet he took as a "given." One young woman, who was about to go off to college, asked her father one day what made the stock market go up and down. He looked at her with amazement and said, "Just because you are growing up to be a woman is no reason you should be stupid." The man simply could not believe that *his* daughter, ready for college and practically weaned on the *New York Times,* could possibly be so ignorant about what seemed to him such a basic financial question. You can be sure this young woman never asked her father that question again, or anything else about money.

The kernel of the problem may be this common misconception. Perhaps most financially astute men cannot imagine that their wives are as ignorant about resource management as they actually are. To such a man, money makes his world and therefore his family's world, go around. As a matter of habit he has paid close attention to money matters for so long, he takes the knowledge for granted. It is as difficult for such a man to comprehend his wife's lack of education about money as it would be for her to realize he couldn't tell a genuinely sick child from one who just wanted a day away from school.

Then, too, on the subject of learning about money, the almost universal mistake is having a husband try to teach his wife about it or almost anything else. You name it—how to drive a car, play bridge, learn to ski or play tennis—spousal education seems to put a great strain on even the best relationships. When the woman goes to a pro for such instruction, no emotional agenda is involved in the education packet, and success is more certain. But because he didn't teach you, and you didn't seek professional counsel on money matters either, you never learned enough about financial management while he was alive.

If you recognize yourself in these few pages, don't feel badly or ashamed. You are not under a life sentence to be ignorant about money. You're not alone and you can do something about it. In fact, you seem to be among the majority of women in their middle years who were married to financially competent men. With no conscious thought at all, and in common with most comfortably married women, you never developed an interest—not to mention an involvement—in the understanding and preservation of your family's money.

In some ways, at least at first, the widow of a prosperous man may be worse off than the widow of a less affluent man who only had to file the *short* income tax form, the 1040A. This form is generally used by couples whose combined income from wages, salaries, tips, and unemployment compensation is under $40,000 a year and whose savings and investments are limited. Their biggest asset is usually their home, on which most of the mortgage has been paid off. If inflation hasn't bumped the house to such a value level that this widow feels she should sell it for profit and move, a widow in this situation probably knows immediately where she stands financially. She knows the amount her husband's pension and life insurance policy will provide for her and what her social security income will be, for they have been closely watching such matters together for years. It is quite likely that she has handled all the financial records and even prepared the tax forms.

But widows who signed the 1040 form, with its itemized deductions, itemized interest and dividend schedules, lists of capital gains and losses, computations of real estate depreciation, interest payments, and self-employment or business expenses, are in another situation and income tax bracket entirely. The packet of yearly tax forms could have been half an inch thick; a mere glance at them brings little understanding of the complexities.

Facing the challenge of learning how to handle the funds you and your husband accumulated over the years of your marriage is difficult. He gained the knowledge needed to handle your family resources gradually. After making a few errors that he didn't say much about, he accomplished money management with skills acquired in the business world.

However, it should be a comfort to you that your husband was not *born* with these skills; he learned them—just as you can. Of course he had more time in which to master them, and he was in an environment that made it easy to do. People around him discussed finance as strangers talk about the weather. A lot of the financial education your husband picked up was informal, though the knowledge was solid.

Now you can learn too. You need to find the knowledge and understanding that will give you a renewed sense of security, based on a confident grasp of your own resources.

Chapter two deals with the emotional adjustments almost any widow has to make in dealing with grief, and the practical matters that appear as she begins to come to grips with her new status and responsibilities. You will realize as you become more involved with the puzzle of your finances that you cannot afford to be ignorant about them—because the best of financial advisors cannot be expected to take as much interest in your welfare and in fulfilling your financial needs as you can. Your consent to transactions that professionals suggest must be *informed* consent.

It is often an agonizing time, which each woman survives at her own pace and in her own way. The second chapter suggests some simple techniques for dealing with practical matters—equipment that can be helpful, methods for creating order out of chaos, especially the chaos of paper that becomes so plentiful and can be very frustrating if not dealt with firmly.

CHAPTER TWO

He's Not Coming Home Again—Ever

Widows are a breed apart, their lives changed without choice from sharing and caring to a strange and solitary existence. Whether your husband's death came with little warning or after months or maybe years of an increasingly debilitating illness, the finality is difficult to grasp. One woman, whose husband weakened daily with double pneumonia that was not responding to treatment, remarked, "Intellectually, I can accept the idea that Charles may die, but not emotionally." That is the hard part.

If your husband's death was slow, a moment may have come during your vigil of his illness when you knew he had gone over into the next dimension, and there would be no return. Perhaps you spoke or uttered a silent leave-taking to the man with whom you shared so much and to whom you had given a generous amount of your life's energies. Perhaps your time together was most of your adult life, or maybe it was just the last few years—as you said goodbye, you felt that chilly draft of change sweep over you.

Close family members were on hand or came quickly, and friends arrived to see if they could help with arrangements that had to be made. The ringing telephone can be maddening. With much coming and going—a virtual frenzy of activity—you feel a buoyancy and slowly absorb the magnitude of difference his death has made. The necessary rituals of death work like an emotional sedative. They dull the impact of loss, delaying the moment of realization until you have time and solitude.

Throughout this period you have been drawing on your reserves, emotional and physical. The most common effect that sets in almost at once is a bewildering inability to remember anything, such as where you put the car keys, whether you had asked someone to notify his close friends who live far away, and if you thanked the friends who brought in dinner for the family members the night he died—ordinary things like that. This forgetfulness will upset you and those people around you who do not understand that temporary memory loss is part of the grieving process. This aberration will not disappear for a while, but you can develop ways of dealing with it. Make notes of anything you want to remember that emerges during a conversation and gather these notes together in a central place, check them off as they are attended to and file them in an envelope or folder. That way the checked-off notes will remind you what has been tended to.

When whatever ceremonial observance you had is over, family members have resumed their lives, and friends no longer hover around trying to anticipate your needs as a way of expressing their love and compassion, you finally have time to begin absorbing what has happened. Slowly it penetrates. He is dead. You will never see him again. And your life has changed forever.

Unspeakable sadness wells up at common things—the sight

of his pajamas and bathrobe hanging in their accustomed place on the back of the bathroom door. His toothbrush and shaving things are still there, and his favorite bottled shampoo stands in the shower caddy. You can't bear looking at them; but you're not actually ready to dispose of them either—they are so intimate. These ordinary objects can bring a flood of tears—perhaps cries of rage. Doing something with these things is a perfect task for someone close to you to take over. Making decisions about the small, personal belongings is for most bereft people the most poignant recognition of death. If someone can spare you that, someone you trust and feel comfortable with who can sensitively select items you might like to keep and dispose of his clothes, shoes, toilet articles, drugs, and other personal paraphernalia in some appropriate way, it is a tremendous expression of caring. This may be hard for someone else to do, but it could be too much for you.

Grief must not be hidden; it must be allowed to run its course. There doesn't seem to be an easy path across the painful terrain of mourning. If this inner torment feels like more than you can handle by yourself and you don't know a minister, priest, or rabbi, telephone your local Hospice and ask for a referral to a grief counselor. Hospice is a nearly nationwide program of service that deals especially with terminally ill people and their families before, during, and after the illness.

Everyone needs help at such a time; someone to listen to you who knows what you are suffering. Expert counsel can bring enormous benefits, and it should be sought with no sense of weakness or shame. No one expects you to be in perfect self-control.

The death of a husband, especially in the middle years when you no longer have the resilience and optimism of youth to pull you through, is an excrutiating experience, especially if your relationship was close and strong. To be a lovingly cared for and protected wife is an enviable situation—until it ends. The first days and weeks are so unreal, your mind does strange things. You may start across a room to get something and forget halfway what it was you were going for. It is hard to get used to saying "I" instead of "we." Often you refer to him in the present, and you may even half expect him to come back, not rationally but subconsciously, at the end of the day.

To face life without the man you were bonded to in a special way is agony enough. After all, you had entrusted your future to him. Fears of your inability to manage alone, of becoming a lesser person now, and of the future that looms bleak and empty encompass you. You wonder how you will survive. This fear is formless, like skating over an icy pond that heaves beneath you, shaking you off balance. The most prosaic things, like marketing or going to the post office, can make you feel a marked woman, as though you carried a placard telling the world your husband has just died. Though you are not wearing black to mark your plight, you still feel specially labeled with the hated word *widow,* as if everyone else could see.

Occasionally you may even feel you are losing your mind. Not true, of course, but you are psychically disoriented in the same way one becomes physically unbalanced when hit by a big wave at the beach. You can't tell which direction to swim in because you don't know which way is up until the wave carries you toward shore and you finally scrape along the rough sand and gratefully gain a foothold. Now you feel the same disorientation, except that it doesn't clear up and go away.

This first period of bereavement is so beset with uncertainties and wild engulfments of grief, it can hardly be stated too strongly that this is *not* the time to make permanent decisions of any magnitude. Getting through each day is difficult enough when you have to handle waves of depression that drag you down and seem to wipe out any effort you make towards some level of normalcy. This is your only concern right now—the adjustment to a day-to-day life that is new and different. The big decisions can wait.

Friends may invite you to their homes for dinner where you will become painfully aware of the last time you went there with your husband. Friends hesitate to talk about him, so to be safe they may not mention him at all, which is wrong. Talk about him if you feel like it, and don't worry that they may think you are going to dwell permanently in the past. If they were friends of his, too, they will feel comfortable about remembering him and will want to share their memories with you. This is the stuff of which friendship is made, the adventures you shared, the special occasions. They will understand if you start to cry or if you are suddenly overcome with a need to go home because that's where you feel safe and close to him.

Try to appear as if you are coping well with your loss, but pretending is foolish. Utilize friendships because your behavior at this stage seems to have its own inexorable rhythm and even wisdom. Ultimately it is a healing process that resolves itself.

It's very important to have at least one person who will be a good listener and who will not remind you that you have already said the same thing at least a dozen times.

"There are no real shortcuts through grief," says Wendy Foster Evans, a Hospice grief counselor. "While each case is different, and each person grieves individually and somewhat differently, there are typically some common states of mind most experience in their adjustment process."

She describes the first phase as *protest;* denial or refusal to face the facts are common reactions. There is anger—anger at

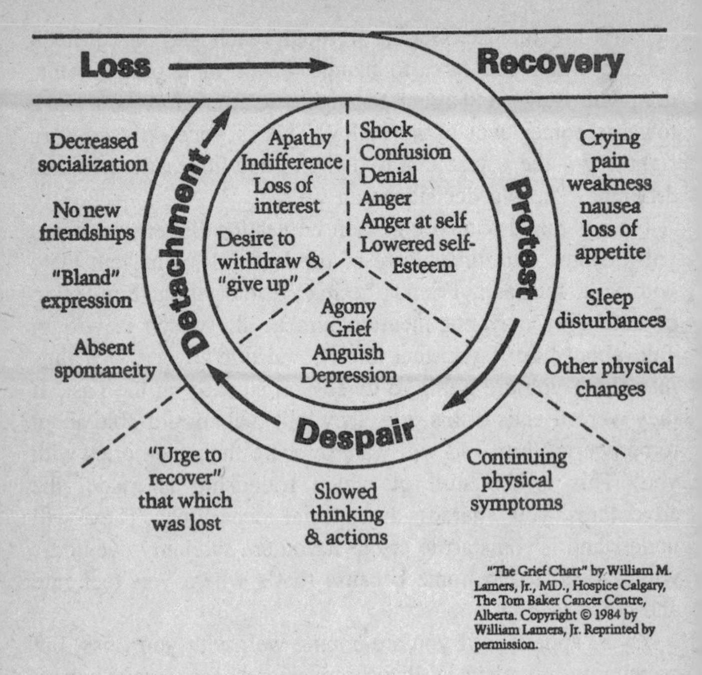

"The Grief Chart" by William M. Lamers, Jr., MD., Hospice Calgary, The Tom Baker Cancer Centre, Alberta. Copyright © 1984 by William Lamers, Jr. Reprinted by permission.

oneself for being in such a mess, guilt that something hadn't been done to prevent it, and even anger at the departed—"How could you leave me like this?" For a complex of reasons, lowered self-esteem follows. Mrs. Evans explained that the loss of a family member disrupts one's whole functioning system so drastically that the survivor feels worthless and indecisive. She also pointed out that in families where children die of cancer, the death of a child causes extreme discord in the majority of marriages. The divorce rate can run from 70 to 90 percent. A death is very divisive, pulling down one's normal expectations and supports. Physical symptoms are varied in the *protest* stage: weeping, pain, nausea, weakness, loss of appetite, insomnia, nightmares, even constipation or colitis are common.

The second state of mind, *despair,* comes when the mind accepts the death as a fact. At this point the survivor often lapses into anguish and depression. Thinking processes are slowed down and one moves ponderously. Thoughts of suicide can occur, and physical symptoms can persist.

The third phase is *detachment*. It comes when the grieving person sinks into apathy and indifference and tends to withdraw from others. The grief-stricken person turns a blank expression toward the world.

Mrs. Evans's colleague, Dr. William Lamers, emphasized that all this is normal. "No matter how strange one's symptoms may seem, they are part of getting through a crisis in life, which—desperate as it may be—can also open the way to inevitable change and growth in the individual, opening up new horizons and opportunities."

Citing some of the things a grieving survivor may try in an attempt to avoid going through this painful process—alcohol, drugs, premature new relationships and abnormal hyperactivity—Lamers and Evans point out that there are particular stress times. Birthdays, anniversaries, and holidays can trigger acute outbursts of emotion. A current loss can also dredge up unresolved feelings from some earlier loss and bring on thoughts of one's own death. And yet reliving the memories of life with a lost family member is a positive though painful phase of the grief experience, part of healing oneself. If a wound is kept covered and unventilated, it will fester and become infected. Like a flesh wound, grief must be aired if it is to heal. Lamers and Evans agree that it takes courage and hard work to get through grief, a necessary healthy process that can be somewhat smoothed when one understands and accepts what is happening. In their experience, almost anything that happens is normal in this situation.

Emotional equilibrium starts to restore itself as you begin to deal with the inescapable tasks suddenly foisted on you. Perhaps the car won't start because the battery is dead. You may still have his car to use, but the problem battery won't recharge itself. Should you call the automobile association to come and "jump" it, or call the service station to sell you a new battery? You have to decide and that starts you thinking. Do you need two cars? Another decision! Should you turn them both in for one new one? Should you run them both as long as they last, carrying insurance on both of them, or should you give one of them to a family member who needs it or sell one? None of these decisions is really earthshaking, but now that no one is around to discuss them with, they may seem monumental.

Letters of condolence from all sorts of people will arrive; you should answer them all no matter how difficult. Some thoughtful letters append a postscript telling you not to bother replying. Letters come from your friends, your husband's friends, and people you never heard him mention. As they pile up, you can get further and further behind and begin to feel burdened just thinking about what has to be done. Fortunately, alternatives to handwritten letters are available. A printed card of thanks for their thoughts of you and the family is acceptable—more so if you sign it. A letter handwritten by a paid temporary secretary who says she is writing on your behalf will also do the job. After all, the idea is to let the senders know that their letters were received and appreciated.

Your limited reservoir of strength needs to be conserved for demands that cannot be delegated. Hiring someone to do the clerical work not only saves you time and energy, it gives you a person with whom to interact about the business of getting on with your life. You will feel better the sooner these mundane details are settled.

It will probably take you longer than usual to do the most

commonplace things, such as looking up telephone numbers or doing the dishes, few as they are. And if you and your husband normally shared a lot of maintenance and gardening work, it will quickly become obvious that you now have twice as much to do around the place. If that seems like a burden, hire someone to help you. This in turn leads you into dealing with another process of adjustment: how you can replace in some fashion the services your husband used to perform as a matter of course. Try to start with the simple things.

If you have the energy and derive any pleasure from it, try doing the job yourself. If it takes more time, energy, and perhaps skills then you have at the moment, or if you don't *want* to do it, perhaps you can find some strong and competent young person to work for you by the hour. If you are not the sort who is disturbed by seeing the garden deteriorate a bit, and you can let things in the house that need fixing go unfixed for a while unless they are serious, let them go. No harm will be done.

Most domestic jobs don't require prompt action, even if your husband had the habit of taking care of them immediately. He probably had his own agenda and some things had priority over others. It takes a long time before a house and garden get into a serious downhill slide.

The results of postponing most chores until you feel more able to deal with them probably won't amount to much. However, if you live in a dry climate, and the sprinkler system suddenly quits, there's no point in letting the whole garden die before you call the person who normally fixes it. Putting off something like that could be very expensive later on.

There are some tricks of adaptation to living alone that help a bit. One widow told me that in order to avoid using a stepladder she always felt uneasy about, she acquired the habit of turning on only those lights whose bulbs she could easily reach when they went out, such as lamps rather than ceiling fixtures, and the light on the stove rather than overhead ones in the kitchen. This may seem a bit extreme, but it made her feel more confident and relaxed. You will come up with your own techniques.

A silent house troubles some women as they realize the only indoor sounds besides the whir of appliances and the creaks a place makes as it ages are the sounds they create themselves. It helps to develop the habit of turning on the stereo, or television, though you never did before. Sounds of other voices or music give a comforting sense.

If you already have a pet, you probably cherish it more than ever now. But if you don't, it might not be a good idea to acquire one before your lifestyle becomes more settled, even though you feel lonely. Unless the need to be needed by another living creature outweighs the responsibility of caring for an animal, put the decision off for a while or else get a pet that someone will be happy to have if you decide later to move or travel to faraway places.

If you live where there are trees and grass, one way to enjoy the pleasure of pets without the responsibilities of ownership is to encourage the smaller wild animals and birds to visit by putting out food. One woman spends some time each morning over coffee watching chipmunks, blue jays, and squirrels vie for position at a bowl of food she puts out. A plastic bird feeder that clings to the window pane with suction cups provides some lively entertainment even if you've never been interested in the habits of birds before. A feeder, plus a sack of wild birdseed, will bring visitors whose behavior is diverting and entertaining.

However, there is no way to shake the feeling that it doesn't matter any longer if you *ever* come home, never mind when. It is very depressing to realize that you are no longer

Number One in anybody's life, that no one depends on you any more for the companionship that made both your lives rewarding. Face it. You get lonely—very lonely—however well you think you are adjusting to a solitary life.

Try an open-minded, experimental approach toward this new and difficult life situation. You may feel waves of anger at your husband for leaving you in a mess like this and you feel like screaming at him. So scream. If nothing else seems to help your sorrow, try a hot bath and stay in it a while. It will relax you and break this mood. Do crossword puzzles or play solitaire, which will absorb your mental energies temporarily. While this helps, there is no panacea for the emotional and physical pain you endure in the beginning.

One woman who received a notice for jury duty not long after her husband died thought of trying to get out of it, but then she decided it might be an interesting experience. She had never served on a jury, and if nothing else, it would take her mind off her own situation. She was among the people called to serve. When the attorney began to question the panel members, she realized she would be asked whether she was married, single, or widowed. Immediately her stomach tightened up at the thought of using that hated word to describe herself—so far she had not said it aloud. When the attorney asked the expected question, she almost shouted "widow" at him and then began to cry. She felt very ashamed, but when the judge asked her if she would like to be excused, she was able to say no. Her composure returned, the brief episode of grief passed, and no one except the judge seemed to have noticed. Soon she was absorbed in the procedures going on and realized she had taken a small step—she had said the word in public.

Most women feel nervous alone in the house at night. Turn on some lights. Robbers reportedly avoid entering an occupied home. Keep doors and any easily accessible windows locked—no neighborhood is safe in today's society and burglar alarms can enhance your peace of mind. Leaving the stereo on often adds security when people are out of their house, and leave lights on if it will be dark when you return.

If you have trouble sleeping through the night and begin to feel depressed, try changing your mood. Like Scarlett O'Hara in *Gone with the Wind,* tell yourself that you will "think about it tomorrow," no matter what "it" is. Almost any dark thought seems less grim in daylight. This isn't an easy thing to do when you're down, but it's not impossible either. Just realize these "night thoughts" are not to be taken seriously.

Some women, now sleeping alone and not concerned about waking their husbands, turn on the light and read. Television stations often have movie reruns going on throughout the night, and there are news programs too. Bedside radios offer programs you may never have known existed before. Call-in talk shows, for one, draw an audience eager to settle the world's problems at 2 o'clock in the morning. It's amazing how many insomniacs there are "out there," or perhaps they are people coming home late or getting up for a dawn stint in a 24-hour restaurant. In any case, everyone seems intent on being heard. The format to these programs is set; only first names are used, and some people are clearly regulars. Most callers are argumentative, though some sound as though they are oversedated. And some people are apparently so lonely to talk with someone, they'd like to spend an hour chatting confidentially while thirty thousand others listen in.

If you like news, many radio stations have excellent programs after midnight, running BBC interviews with reporters just back from wherever the world's current trouble spot is or in-depth news analysis that provides a refreshing change from the brief headline type of daytime news. Many thoughtful programs are aired by metropolitan stations, and they carry almost no advertising breaks to interrupt. If you fall asleep in the process, that's wonderful!

Finally, there is the common matter of guilt feelings. According to many of the women I talked with, guilt is an almost tangible shadow, clouding the circumstances of their husband's deaths. Usually, of course, the guilt is totally unfounded, and it finally evaporates as rational thinking takes over. However, while they are dominant, guilt feelings can hinder a woman's re-entry into the world of successful survivors. An example of this is a young woman named Audrey who was married to an attorney who occasionally played polo on Sunday afternoons for his community team in the mid-South. Very early one Sunday morning, Audrey wakened from a dream in which her husband was standing beside an ethereal figure in a long flowing gown. In the dream, her husband spoke to her clearly and gently, saying, ''I'm sorry darling, but I have to leave you now.''

Audrey woke up crying, and she wakened her husband to tell him about the dream. He brushed it off and teased her about having too much wine at a dinner party the night before. He comforted her before going back to sleep, but she was wakeful the rest of the night. During breakfast he answered a phone call asking him to fill in for another player on that week's polo team and he agreed to play. When she heard about it, Audrey was terrified and begged him not to go. She argued in vain, he left to drive to the polo field, and laughed at her. ''What on earth's the matter with you? Are you afraid you're going to be a widow?'' ''Yes!'' she cried out. He laughed again, kissed her and drove off. That afternoon, while Audrey watched, his horse threw him—he broke his neck and died instantly.

For the next few years, Audrey was haunted by the feeling that she should have done something, *anything*—even set fire to the house—to detain him. She felt guilty that she had had a premonition and hadn't exerted herself enough to prevent the accident. Eventually, Audrey went to a psychic a friend had told her about. The psychic convinced Audrey that she indeed had had a premonition of an event, but an event that could no more be prevented from happening than could the birth of a baby that has gone to term. Once convinced that her dream was precognition, foreknowledge of an event about to occur, Audrey was able to accept her husband's death as inevitable, and her guilt left her.

Another woman named Joan agonized for a long time that she had not talked her husband out of an elective surgical procedure his regular physician had refused to authorize because the husband had had a series of small strokes. His doctor felt the risks outweighed the possible benefit of the surgical remedy. However, her husband was a person who made his own decisions independently of his wife or anyone else. He found another doctor who was sanguine about the outcome, and the surgery was performed. Her husband died in the hospital a few days later of a massive brain hemorrhage, and his widow still feels she should have persuaded the second doctor that her husband was not a fit candidate for any sort of surgery, by telling the doctor specifics about her husband's condition that he had undoubtedly failed to mention. She also feels she might have asked the first doctor to intervene and blames herself that she was not assertive enough to prevent an operation that she felt carried a great risk.

A final example is Sally, a widow who grieves that she should have been more insistent that her husband take care of a virus infection each of them had, by staying home and in bed as she was doing. He was a person who hated to break business appointments or social engagements as long as he was *able* to keep them—able in this case meaning capable of getting around even with a low fever. A few days later, his doctor put him in the hospital with double pneumonia. None of the miracle drugs worked, and finally his heart gave out while the fever raged. Like Joan, Sally carries a heavy extra burden because she feels she could have done something more to impose her will. Saddest of all, while in the hospital, her husband told her he knew he wouldn't be there if only he had taken her advice. This sensitive, conscientious woman feels she failed in a responsibility, a flagrant violation of the obligations prescribed in marriage vows.

These very normal reactions are part of the syndrome of grief. They are a natural part of the anger and denial that torment an anguished woman who feels abandoned by the man she loved, the man she depended on for material and emotional sustenance. Without him her ongoing life may seem an empty and useless struggle.

We all recognize the inevitable truth of the Old Testament book of Ecclesiastes. "To everything there is a season, and a time to every purpose under heaven . . . a time to be born and a time to die." Regardless of the truth of it, the emotional acceptance comes much harder, and it takes its own measure of time.

"We live in a culture that until recently has been death-denying," says Mary Taverna, a Hospice executive director. "People feel uncomfortable with an individual who is grieving. They don't know how to act, what to say or do. There is pressure on the bereaved to snap out of it and pretend they are all right." Wendy Foster Evans, mentioned earlier, observes that there is not much leeway in our society for grieving. Some people don't want to see other people in pain. They feel awkward unless the grieving person acts as though everything is fine.

The therapy of work, especially the demands of an unfamiliar sort of work, such as the settlement of your husband's estate or the perplexing question of what to do with his life insurance money, can provide the sort of distraction, even absorption, that gives your mind and emotions a rest from the ever-present fact that you have now begun a new life—alone.

The healing process of this necessary work therapy begins with the next chapter.

CHAPTER THREE

First Steps on Your Own

Your private emotional world is likely to be invaded by a phone call from the lawyer who drew up your husband's will asking that you and any family members who might be interested come to his office because he would like to read you the will.

With your relatives as shepherds, you numbly enter his office at the appointed hour and endeavor to listen. It soon becomes impossible to understand what he is reading, droning on page after page in legal language that might as well be Latin. When finished reading, if the lawyer is at all sensitive, he will give you a rough translation of the will in common English and a few simple instructions about what is to come next. He will tell you what he needs from you to proceed with settling your husband's estate.

For the purposes of this book, I am assuming you have been named executrix of the estate. The process is remarkably informative, and the experience of being executrix is the best possible way to begin learning about financial management. The lawyer should give you, as executrix, a written list of what you should do and in what order. The procedures would be the same no matter who is executor.

You will be asked to produce a death certificate and your husband's financial records: his checkbooks and passbooks for bank accounts, life insurance policies, other insurance policies, stock and bond certificates, deeds of trust involving any real estate holdings, the deed to the house, automobile pink slips, last year's income tax return, military papers, if any, property tax records, the bills for his last illness, details of any health insurance coverage, pension plan documents, and any of his personal bills that have come in. You will be able to find all these papers if you follow your instincts because there are only so many places they could be—his desk, his office files, his filing place at home, and the safe deposit box.

While zeroing in on these chores, some nagging questions may begin to depress you: "What do I have to live on?" "How much money is available, and when will it arrive?" "How much do I *need* to live on and will there be enough?" It is with discouraging frequency that you realize you have no answers to any of these questions, and no one else seems to be able to tell you, either.

Meanwhile, bills have indeed been coming in—bills related to his illness, personal bills of his and yours, perhaps a real estate or property tax notice that has become overdue. That bill tells you how much you should have paid had you done it on time and what you now have to pay with the penalty added. A sizeable homeowner's insurance bill may have come, but you don't know whether to pay it or not because your checking account is getting low. Yet if you don't, that coverage giving you essential protection will lapse. You have to pay it somehow.

During this rocky period, your husband's insurance agent

has probably learned of the death, and called or written to tell you that a supply of cash is readily available as soon as you return the forms he will send you to fill out. Should you not hear from the agent, nor even know who he is, hunt for a file labeled *Insurance*. It may contain policies of various sorts, but you are going after life insurance only, and the agent's name and address will be on the policy somewhere.

After you locate the file, you might notice another symptom of grief. You can look at strange documents for minutes at a time and not be able to take in one bit of the written information. That's to be expected. Your mind is numb. If you can't find what you want, call on a friend for help. Give your friend the file and chances are a more nimble mind will quickly produce the information you want—the agent's name and phone number.

Call him and watch things happen! The agent will ask you to provide him with a death certificate, too, and he will also tell you where to get it. The actual procedures necessary for such a document have been underway since the day your husband died. At that time the attending physician signed a form stating that he had died, when, and of what causes. Through long-established channels, the information went its way, and is now available to you in the form the insurance company, the lawyer and several other people need. Obtain at least a dozen certified copies altogether to be attached to various documents. Each has to be an original—photocopies are not acceptable. They are obtained for a nominal fee from your county health department.

The insurance agent or agents—if your husband had more than one policy—can quickly tell you how much money you are due to receive after you return the forms they send you. The amount could be less than the face value of the policy if your husband had borrowed against it. In a period of high interest rates at banks, borrowing on life insurance policies at a low rate stipulated in the policy became a popular way of acquiring capital to invest at higher rates. In this case, of course, the policies' final payments to beneficiaries are reduced by the amount borrowed against them. The agent will be able to give you the specific details.

The total coming to you very shortly is likely to be larger than any amount of money you have had in your possession at one time before. The size of the check will very likely ease your mind, but it will also raise more worries and questions because you have no idea what to do with that much cash besides depositing it in the bank. A large amount of money should not be left idle for more than a brief period. You can postpone most decisions for a while, but this one should not be delayed because money in any quantity is a valuable servant. Put to work, it can improve the quality of your life by increasing the amount of disposable income available to you. But you have to ask the questions and then make the decisions about *how* to put the money to work—you are now the one in charge.

You should keep in mind two fundamental concepts. Whatever you decide to do with the money, (1) it should be earning as much interest as it safely can (that is, making more money for you), and (2) it should be liquid—readily available to you in cash form to draw upon. This availability is important because you don't yet know how much you will need nor when you will need it, and you probably won't know for the first year. Generally speaking, money in a passbook savings account at a bank for savings and loan association doesn't do much for you these days. It pays only 5¼ or 5½ percent or what amounts to $55 interest per year earned on a deposit of $1,000.

Keeping the two basic requisites in mind, by all means talk the situation over with your local bank manager. Banking is a regulated industry, but many changes have occurred among commercial banks and savings and loans so that they have numerous options beyond a simple passbook account. It may be that one of them can offer you a program that meets your requirements with a rate of return equal to or more than the money market funds discussed below.

CAUTION: The lifting of many restrictions on banks is relatively recent. In order to attract money market fund investors, some banks are advertising higher interest rates. These are subject to change and there are often "hidden" charges. Be sure to read the "fine print."

Both banks and savings and loans will emphasize the *safety* of depositing funds with them because each account is insured up to $100,000 by an agency of the federal government. These institutions offer a variety of accounts in addition to "demand" deposits, or the 5¼ or 5½ percent passbook savings accounts, several with the funds available on demand, or nearly so. You can also choose to leave your money in for a specified period of time and usually earn a higher interest rate. This is called a time deposit or a certificate of deposit—a "CD" in the banking business. However, it means you have committed your money to them for a period of time—a month, three months, two years or whatever—and you will have to pay a penalty if you draw it out before the date agreed on, its maturity.

You may choose to open several accounts, putting money you do not need in CDs, while maintaining a supply of ready cash in a regular passbook account or an interest-bearing checking account. That way you can earn higher interest on some of the money. If you have $100,000 you do not have immediate need of and you want to put it in a bank or savings and loan in a "Jumbo" account, it will earn the highest going rate. Ask.

Another option is to lend your money to a corporation for a short period of time. In return you get a document called commercial paper, available for loans of $25,000 and up from a stockbrokerage firm or your bank. However, these are not insured by the U.S. Government, so ask about their safety. Some well-known companies have weakened lately.

Money market funds, including many of those in banks and savings and loan associations, generally pay a high rate of interest, and you can withdraw money from them almost as easily as if it were in a checking account. Money market funds automatically deposit the interest earned directly into your account with them, and you receive a monthly statement. If you leave the interest in to accumulate, it will earn interest as well. Although only the funds run by banks or savings and loans are insured up to $100,000, judging by the billions deposited with them of uninsured funds, they enjoy a high rate of public confidence. Their importance to you is that once the funds are deposited, you are issued a book of checks that you can use as you would any other check, except that generally they cannot be written for less than $500. You can use these checks to pay the monthly mortgage or your property taxes—or anything you owe that is more than $500. If you decide to use this particular sort of investment, you can keep track of your fund's current rate of interest by looking in the financial pages of your local newspaper on Fridays. They vary their rates almost in unison. Most money market funds require an initial deposit of at least $2,500 to buy into them. (See chart.)

Money market funds are generally regarded as both a convenient and productive "parking place" for funds while long-term investment decisions are being made. Though they give a good return in a period of high interest rates, your capital has no chance for growth unless you leave the interest in to accumulate, just like a savings account. The return they provide is assured for only one day at a time. It may go up one day and down the next, depending on capricious interest

Money Market Mutual Funds

New York (AP) — NASD Inc.'s money market funds summary as of December 4

	Assets ($million)	Average Maturity	7 day Yield	30 day Yield
AMEV Fd	74	28	7.16	7.15
AARP	67	73	7.08	7.12
ActiveAssetGovt	165	53	7.07	7.39
ActiveAssetMoney	2156	45	7.40	7.39
AlexBrownCash	631	26	7.38	7.39
AlexBrownGovt	145	38	7.27	7.29
AllianceCapRes f	867	34	7.07	7.07
AllianceGovtRes f	185	26	6.98	6.94
AmerGnlMoney a	34	64	7.48	7.59
AmerCapResrv a	214	44	7.27	7.42
AmNatl	13	17	7.42	7.41
AutCsh	949	35	7.58	7.53
AutGvt	1361	46	7.33	7.30
BLC Cash	40	16	7.00	6.91
BabsonMoneyMkt	60	23	7.18	7.15
BirrWilson	54	22	6.63	6.63
BostonCoCash	225	52	7.32	7.30
BostonCoGovt	20	47	6.75	6.76
BullBearDollr	81	82	6.92	6.97
CBA MoneyFd	15	53	7.38	7.37
CIMCO	10	43	7.44	7.40
CalvertSocial af	50	24	7.22	7.24
CAM Fd	36	19	6.85	6.93
CapitalCashMgt	112	13	7.47	7.47
CapitalPreservFd	1864	52	6.96	6.74
CapitlPreserv II	522	1	7.03	7.17
CapT MM	171	26	7.28	7.22
CardinalGvtSec	416	12	7.54	7.50
CarnegieGvtSecur	....	39	7.86	....
CashAssets	69	16	7.22	7.33
CashEquivM	4926	22	7.45	7.41
CashEquivIntGvt	526	17	7.28	7.36
CashMgmtTrAm a	544	18	7.53	7.52
CashPlusFedl	106	42	7.49	7.37
CashPlusMMkt	293	41	7.85	7.81
CashResrvMgmt a	3957	27	7.74	7.57
CentennialGvtTr	71	1	7.12	7.08
CentennialMMTr	162	38	7.88	7.86
ChurchillCashRsv	123	13	7.45	7.45
CignaCash	34	41	7.23	7.37
CignaMMkt b	....	51	7.36	7.41
ColonialMMkt	10	18	6.93	6.95
ColumbDivIncm af	435	30	7.14	7.13
CommandGovt	102	33	7.26	7.26
CommandMny a	1104	37	7.42	7.40
CompositeCshMg a	138	22	6.91	6.88
CortlandGeneral	136	19	7.18	7.14
CortlandUSGvt	27	43	6.58	6.60
CurrentInterest	868	32	7.15	7.14
CurrentIntUSGvt	83	32	6.99	7.01
DBL MM Portfolio	1348	59	7.27	7.30
DBL GvtSec	219	63	7.23	7.23
DailyCashAccum	2306	39	7.34	7.34
DailyDollar	226	34	7.19	7.20
DailyIncomeFd	460	26	7.29	7.26
DailyPassportCsh f	621	39	7.04	7.03
DWitterSearLqd	6418	46	7.38	7.43
DWitrSearUS	422	53	6.97	6.91
DelawareCashRes f	1386	33	7.26	7.27
DelawareTr	54	92	6.84	6.84
DreyfInstl	580	38	7.59	7.58
DreyfLiqAssets	8200	43	7.46	7.45
DreyGovtSeries	1028	81	7.44	7.42
DryInstGovt	1036	94	7.50	7.51
DreyfMMktSer	648	54	7.52	7.50
EGT MoneyMkt f	68	44	6.99	6.96
EatonVanceCshMg	211	31	7.30	7.26
EquitableMoney	217	40	7.86	7.88
FBL MoneyMkt	27	19	6.57	6.53
FahnstckDaily	132	34	7.12	7.12
FederatedMasterTr	2845	40	7.63	7.62
FidelityCashRes	4094	39	7.42	7.43
FidelityDlyIncm b	2531	38	7.26	7.36
FidelGovtPortf	1047	32	7.86	7.82

TAX EXEMPT

	Assets ($million)	Average Maturity	7 day Yield	30 day Yield
ActvAsetTxFr	720	56	4.68	4.45
AllianceTaxEx	394	65	4.64	4.55
BenhamCalTxFre	112	74	4.43	4.27
BenhamNtlTaxFr	31	88	4.99	4.84
BostonCo	98	74	4.93	4.75
CalvertTxFree	316	79	4.83	4.77
CapitlTTax	28	62	4.70	4.40
CarnegieTxFree	....	85	4.87	....
CentennialTaxEx	228	53	4.46	4.28
CommandTax	385	69	4.64	4.48
CortlandTaxFree c	23	47	4.15	3.80
DBL TaxFree	323	93	4.73	4.60
DailyTaxFree c	1107	68	4.71	4.69
DeanWitrSears	640	61	4.83	4.61
DelawareTaxFree	56	85	4.64	4.48
DreyTxExempt c	2349	73	4.83	4.68
EmpireTaxFree	60	79	4.56	4.42
FederatedTxFree c	3628	44	4.73	4.59
FidelityTxExmt c	3109	67	5.01	4.88
FstInvstTaxEx	37	95	4.73	4.44
FstTrstTaxFree	24	105	4.52	4.22
FranklnTaxExmt c	89	45	5.04	5.00
FundTaxFree	28	88	4.57	4.35
GnTxExmptMM	345	92	4.71	4.59
IDS TaxFree c	....	85	4.70	....
KidderPeabTx	506	62	4.83	4.60
LandmarkTaxFree	139	56	4.53	4.39
LehmanTax	428	56	4.84	4.70
LexingtonTaxFr c	84	89	4.78	4.60
LiquidGreenTx	17	63	4.93	4.69
MarinerTax	47	68	5.06	4.67
McDnldTaxEx	67	91	4.84	4.65
MerrLyn CMA	5315	67	4.64	4.43
MerrLyInst	213	52	4.90	4.63
MdwstGrp	81	99	5.32	5.37
MoneyMgtPlus	54	92	4.48	4.62
NatTaxExempt	39	91	4.95	4.80
NeubergBermTxFr	81	81	4.82	4.56
NuveenTxFrRs	1977	43	4.87	4.74
NuveenTxFrAct	182	35	4.84	4.65
NuveenTxFree	166	45	4.69	4.54
PacifHorzMMkt	45	62	4.30	4.09
ParkAveNY	143	57	4.53	4.27
PrudBacheTax	....	57	4.55	4.45
RMA TaxFree	576	72	4.72	4.43
ReserveConn	94	89	4.60	4.41
ReserveInterst	187	82	4.42	4.41
ReserveNY	60	85	4.02	4.02
RothschldEx	80	32	4.28	4.20
RowePriceTxEx cf	920	87	4.76	4.62
StClairTaxFree	41	75	4.99	4.87
ScudderTaxFr cf	270	13	4.50	4.16
SeligmanTaxEx	32	8	4.92	4.71
ShearsonDailyTax	482	71	4.72	4.38
Shearson FMA Mun	693	72	4.75	4.39
SteinRoeTaxEx	162	42	4.69	4.54
TaxExpt c	734	59	4.73	4.52
TaxFreeCashRsv	115	52	4.95	4.68
TaxFreeFund	....	48	4.48	....
TaxFreeInstrum	940	48	4.63	4.52
TaxFreeMoney c	635	33	4.77	4.53
ThomsonMcTaxExmpt	179	90	4.88	4.62
TrustFdsEastern	438	77	4.89	4.74
TrustFdsWestern	211	70	4.73	4.59
TuckerAntTaxEx	114	91	4.72	4.66
USAA TaxEx	97	88	5.14	5.04
UST MasterTaxEx	152	37	5.11	4.94
ValueLineTaxEx	20	106	4.37	4.18
VangMuniBdMM cf	698	66	4.88	4.72

a—Yield includes capital gains or losses. b—Fixed charges vary yield based 4.39

(Reprinted by permission: Tribune Media Services, Inc.)

rates. A money market fund is something like a mutual fund, discussed in chapter six, "Welcome to Wall Street," in that the money you deposit is added to other people's money. Thus lumped together, the resulting fund can be invested by its directors in sums of $100,000 or more and so qualify for the highest interest available.

Money market funds are invested in a broad but reliable variety of government or corporate securities. If you are interested in finding out more about money market funds, ask your bank or savings and loan, watch for advertisements in the financial sections of your newspaper, call a stockbrokerage firm about them or ask one of your own or your husband's friends. Many have 800 phone numbers.

Your decision about how to put the insurance money to work until you are ready to set some long-term investment goals depends on how much you have and how much you think you need to keep on hand. To get an idea of how much can be earned at present interest rates, assume you want to take $10,000 and put it to work. Ask your banker how much it could earn per year according to his suggestions, and compare that with the information you get about money market funds. And compare the *availability* of the money for expenses you probably still can't estimate.

When your immediate money worries are taken care of for a while, it is a good idea—a necessity, really—for you to create an orderly method of handling other tasks that are unfamiliar to you. A tape recorder can be your portable secretary and serve you well. If you have to rely on just your memory during consultations you will have with professionals, you will probably forget a lot of what they tell you. No one can hold quantities of new information together right away. Using a recorder to tape the sessions, you can play the tapes back in the quiet of your home and make notes then about the precise details you have to attend to. When using a tape recorder, however, it is essential to mark the tapes with identifying names and dates so you will know later which one you want to listen to without spending frustrating hours going through the whole lot.

Tape recorders come small enough to be carried in your purse. You may want to borrow one from a friend for a while until you get the knack of using it. When you do buy one, get an extension cord so you can use it plugged in when possible. Though they run on batteries as well, batteries can give out when least expected; or worse, there may be enough power to turn the tape but not enough to record—something one discovers too late. Before you are the confident relaxed woman you will become, you will probably need at least a dozen blank tapes. You won't want to erase an early tape you made in the lawyer's office, for instance, until you become more sure of yourself. Though they erase simply by recording over them again, your growing tape library can give you instant access to important information any time you want it. Sixty-minute tapes are the most convenient.

To keep estate matters from getting mixed up with your personal bills, letters, and whatever else you keep in your desk, it is a good idea to organize a new work space just for estate matters. If possible set aside a different desk or a card table to be used only for settling your husband's estate and keeping your own and the estate's financial records. Do this before your visit to the lawyer with the papers he requires. It is a good device for feeling that you're starting off on the right foot.

A file drawer is essential. You can get a sturdy cardboard one that works well at a stationery store. They are made to hold standard size (8½ × 12) folders. You will also need a dozen legal-size manila folders, a box of paper clips, some sharp pencils, and a lot of inexpensive paper to use as work sheets. You might also want to buy a large notebook to record your expenses, income, and other information. This is all data you will want to have available later when your accountant prepares an income tax return for you.

Once your filing system is established, you will find it easier to keep your work place orderly if you immediately take care of each piece of mail as it arrives, doing whatever is required. This will also give you a sense of confidence that things are being taken care of and you aren't forgetting anything.

Some dividend checks may have arrived. They should be deposited in your account or your husband's estate account. Since the estate account may not be opened yet (it is discussed in the next chapter on executing your husband's will), as you deposit each check, make a record of it in a book that you set up for the purpose of recording your income and mark the estate deposits with your husband's initials. If you are using an 8 × 10½ notebook, a very simple method is to head each page with the month and the year, and list each check showing the date deposited, and source of the check, and to whom it was made out. At the far right of the page, put the amount.

Whatever system you may use later, this method will make it possible to trace every check, keep the funds straight, and make it easy for you to give the accountant, or whomever will prepare your tax returns, the information both he and the lawyer will need. Certified public accountants charge anywhere from $75 to $150 an hour, and even though that cost is tax deductible, the more work you do the less the accountant has to do, thus reducing your bill. Another important reason to keep these detailed records is that they will help you understand where your money comes from and eventually where it goes—the ebb and flow of your own finances.

Every situation and every widow's capacity to learn is different. If you can regard what lies ahead as a new course of study in a field that has suddenly become very important to you, you will find a lot of the information and the tools you need in this book. You will also find the help you need by learning to ask the right questions and how to deal with trained professionals once you have selected them. The place to start is with the realization that you are a beginner, and there's no shame in that. You may have your own well-developed areas of expertise and still feel like it is the first day of kindergarten when you sit down to talk with your banker.

One woman, now a widow, was knowledgeable in the field of art. She was a museum docent and had assembled a fine art collection of her own over the years. When she suddenly found herself alone, her biggest fear was that their home—richly decorated with her excellent collection—might burn down and she would discover too late that the fire insurance policy covering the artworks had lapsed.

Because she knew the worth of what she had—a valuable collection that represented substantial tangible security to her—she greatly feared that this one thing of value she understood might be destroyed. But she didn't know where to turn. She only knew that her husband had taken care of the insurance, and she didn't know the name of the company, the agent, nor where the policy might be. The widow was in a state of barely controlled panic until one day a bill appeared in the mail with all the information she wanted. "I didn't even know that insurance companies sent bills," she admitted with some embarrassment. She never paid a bill so fast and with such a sigh of relief. Stupid? No, she was an intelligent, highly educated woman who was simply confronted with a totally unfamiliar situation. In her harried state of mind, she was quite unable to think her way through to a practical solution, such as looking back through her husband's checkbook register for the agent's name.

As you ponder the last few months, you may wonder if you and your husband could have done anything that would have helped you avoid so much floundering and feeling both helpless and vulnerable when he died. The answer is yes, but it is too rarely done, especially by more affluent couples who could profit the most. And that is unfortunate. The subject of death, the contemplation of it in a serious way, is something people seem to fear as though it might become a self-fulfilling prophecy. Estate planning—a new term for an old responsibility—could and should be handled well ahead of time by both husband and wife. That way the woman is already well-educated when it is necessary for her to act.

According to one statistical analyst, most women can expect to be widows for eighteen years of their lives. Whatever the figure, if you were younger than your husband, the statistics were against you ever fulfilling Robert Browning's poetic dream to, "Grow old along with me, the best is yet to be, the last of life for which the first was made." In almost all marriages these days, the woman outlives the man by several years at least, unless her husband was years younger than she.

Once every year it would have been a very good idea to meet with your husband formally, preferably with his financial advisor as well, to go over your financial situation. Both of you could have discussed your investments and any changes in your family life that might have necessitated alterations in your current wills, and agreed on any other actions or changes that might have been beneficial. In the process, you would gradually have learned terminology and management concepts that you are now struggling to master under pressure.

With today's vastly increased number of two-income families, you are probably among the last generation of women who will face the death of a spouse without some certainty of what your financial resources are. And you can certainly encourage your still-married friends to do what you and your husband did not do, though it is a touchy subject. However, it does no good to dwell on what you both might have done. It's not much comfort to know that hindsight is 20/20 while no one has yet figured out the optical correction for perfect foresight. You are where you are.

You have begun to take care of estate matters, process and account for checks, set up a work space and filing system, and you're keeping accurate financial records. Next you will wade into the day-to-day work of being executrix. Before you get into that in the next chapter, you should know that Congress gave you a big break when it passed the Economic Recovery Tax Act of 1981, which became effective January 1, 1982. Under this law, all gifts and bequests between you and your husband—called interspousal transactions—can be made tax free, and the marital deduction is now unlimited. The marital deduction is the amount of her husband's estate under the will a widow is entitled to without having to pay a tax. Prior to 1982, the tax-free amount was $50,000 or 50 percent of the adjusted gross estate, whichever was greater. In the financial sense, gross means the total before any deductions or allowances are taken out. Net means after the deductions are taken. Whatever comes to you from your husband's estate now will amount to a good deal more than it might have a few years ago. The state in which you reside may still feel it is entitled to some financial consideration, however, so your lawyer will inform you about local laws. California eliminated the interspousal tax as of January 1981.

CHAPTER FOUR

Where There's a Will There's a Lawyer

The first step in this new and unquestionably adult education program begins when you prepare for your first solo appointment with the lawyer handling your husband's estate. You probably only vaguely recall a few highlights from the family gathering with him that took place when he read the will very soon after your husband died. Your overall impression is that everything was left to you, more or less, but you were in a state of shock at the time. Unless another lawyer was one of the family members, all eyes were glazed over, and every mind confused by the time the reading was finished, especially if the will provided for children with A and B trusts, which will be explained later on.

At the time you and your husband made out your wills, he may have explained many of the provisions to you. Though you probably did not understand much of it then, you didn't care to probe too deeply because the time when you would need to make sense of it seemed far over the horizon of your thoughts. It was a prospect too unpleasant to think about.

Settling his estate is the first big piece of business you have to attend to in your new situation. Family members have all left to resume the sequence of their own lives, and you probably feel confused and very alone. For this appointment, make sure you at least *look* competent. It will help your morale. Do the best you can. What you may feel (not unexpectedly), is that your mind is a wooly mess.

Put on the suit you bought last year to go on a business trip with your husband. You may notice it fits better than it did because you've lost some weight. A small plus. A last glance in the mirror tells you that you look a great deal better than you feel, as you pick up your husband's briefcase containing the documents the lawyer asked you to bring. You also have a tape recorder with two hours of fresh tapes ready to record this conference. That way you will have the lawyer's next batch of instructions so you can review them whenever you need to.

En route to the lawyer's office you realize that this is the first excursion beyond the grocery story and the post office you have taken by yourself. Somehow, it brings back a flood of memories, and tears come quickly. By now you know that if you wait, the feeling will pass. So give it a few minutes, even if it makes you a little late for your appointment. Try diverting yourself in some way—walk into a florist shop, a bakery, a book shop, or just study the passersby a few minutes—anything to give yourself a chance to switch emotional gears.

Once settled beside the attorney's desk, get the recorder working and make sure to press the *record* button along with the play button.

Now you begin the process of executing your husband's will. It is required that you do this "in accordance with the state and federal laws" as well as the provisions the will stipulated. These are spelled out in the forty or so pages of language that seemed endlessly repetitive and meaningless to you when you first heard it read.

However, the attorney explains the will to you this time in much clearer terms, and he explains that you, as executrix, have four primary duties to perform. First, you must gather tha assets of the estate. This means you must make a list of everything your husband owned by himself, in a partnership with others, and with you. Whatever he owned by himself is termed *separate* property. Whatever he owned with you is *community property* or is owned in *joint tenancy.* Whatever he owned with a partner or partners is usually called *tenants-in-common*.

After you have made a complete listing of the estate's assets or resources, your next job is to pay the estate's debts. Your third task will be to pay the death taxes, if any, and there is a legal time limit on this. Fourth and finally, you are to distribute the remaining assets in accordance with your husband's will.

- *Gather the assets*
- *Pay the estate's debts*
- *Pay the death taxes, if any*
- *Distribute the assets according to the will*

Your husband's estate became an entity, a separate *thing*, when your husband died. It has a life of its own until everything is settled. This is not necessarily a short time; a year and a half is about average, provided there are no lawsuits involved.

Next the attorney will explain the kind of accounting you must keep to satisfy the court that you have properly performed these four duties under the law. You don't have to take an accounting course for this, but you will need to record the expenses of the estate, such as nurses', doctors' and hospital bills, funeral expenses, and any bills of your husband's. You must also record the estate's income, as mentioned in the last chapter: any checks made out to your husband or to you and him together. Also include the ongoing major expenses of the house, if you owned it together, such as the mortgage payments and sizeable repairs, insurance payments and real estate or property taxes. The lawyer will give you the specifics.

While the lawyer is describing for you the orderly procedure for executing the will—it is choreographed almost like a ballet—be sure to interrupt to ask questions if a term doesn't make any sense or you are not sure what a certain procedure entails. He is retained by the estate to perform these services, just as you are as executrix, and it is his job to make things clear to you. He won't know what you don't understand unless you tell him, for every client he sees has a different familiarity with legal terminology. This is the point at which you have to stop being embarrassed because you don't understand something and ask to have it made clear. Things will go more smoothly for both of you in the long run if you do this on the spot.

The lawyer will probably begin by telling you that he will prepare some forms regarding the probate of the estate, which he will file with the court. Shortly after the date of filing, there will be a court hearing that you probably won't have to attend. The court will then admit the will to probate and appoint the person named in the will—you or someone else—as executrix or executor. Assuming it is you, you will receive copies of all these documents as they are filed, and they should be kept in chronological order in a single file folder.

You may be aware that there are books around on the subject of how to avoid probate. This is probably not possible in your case, but you can always ask. Unless your husband's estate is very moderate and consists only of property he held jointly with you, which means it simply passes to you now, you probably won't be able to avoid probate. An example of a moderate estate is half ownership with you in your home, a pension, and perhaps a few securities. Anything more complicated requires probate proceedings and the services of a lawyer.

After the will is admitted to probate and you officially become executrix, the court issues what are called letters testamentary. These are forms that are stamped by the court clerk, and they show that the court has in fact appointed you executrix, giving you authority to proceed with the business on which you embarked.

Your next step is to close out your husband's previous bank accounts and open new ones in your name followed by your title, executrix. You will then reregister securities that were his separate property in your name as executrix. You will also reregister all other securities, that is, stocks and bonds, that you and your husband owned together in joint tenancy or as community property into your name alone. The lawyer will explain how to do this.

As you go about your job as executrix, gathering the assets of the probate estate, you will make a list of everything your husband owned as his separate property: that is, what he brought to your marriage or received as a gift or inheritance afterwards; next, list what he owned as a tenant-in-common with a relative or partner. As you produce the documents, the lawyer will explain the category they belong in. Finally, you will list everything he owned jointly with you. This information is on property deeds, stock certificates, and registered bonds. You will also be expected to list any property your husband may previously have put into a trust.

Questions will inevitably arise in your mind as you start making a record of these assets and carrying out your other duties as executrix. Don't worry about asking them, since you are probably dealing with the attorney on a fixed-fee basis. Ask about that. This may be the only time in your life you will be using a lawyer's services in this fashion. His fee will probably be the same as yours for your services as executrix, and both are payable by the estate. If you need to ask questions, don't hesitate. Telephone the lawyer if you need to, his meter will not be running, but do take notes on his answers to help you organize your work more efficiently. If your husband did business with a large law firm, there is usually a particular person who handles estates for the office and with whom you will be working. Do not be shy of talking with the lawyer your husband saw, if there is something you want to know that is not being answered. He may be a senior partner who knows more about your husband's business than the one who is actually handling the estate.

One of the first things you will need to investigate is your husband's safe deposit box at the bank. If it is sealed on his death, the attorney will tell you when you can have access to it. To do this, you will need his key and that of the bank, which the bank has. It takes both to open it. If you don't find a key marked with a number, bring whatever keys you can find and can't identify to the bank. Bank personnel can spot a safe deposit key quickly. If you absolutely cannot find it, the key can be replaced for a sum. Once the box is open, make a list of all the non-cash assets—stocks, bonds, and deeds—that have to do with your husband; list any cash, too. You may find some *bearer* bonds there. These have coupons attached which are cashed at a bank semiannually. These especially, of all the papers you may find, should never be out of safekeeping because they are the property of the person who holds them. Hence the name, bearer bonds. The safe deposit box may also contain personal effects such as coins or his grandfather's gold pocket watch. Everything that is his should be listed. You will probably be accompanied to the safe deposit box by a "representative of the court."

At the same time you might also want to make a list of

your separate property in the box, such as jewelry, coins, and any stocks or bonds that are yours. You may have forgotten they were there, and you will want such a list later on.

The list of his assets is then reported to the court by the lawyer, and the court will issue its order, fixing the tax, if any.

It is the task of the executrix to make sure that there is ample insurance on the house if half of it belongs to your husband's estate. In these days of escalated real estate values, your house insurance may not realistically cover its replacement cost. You will need to discuss the coverage you have with the insurance agent who wrote the policy.

Unless you are quite familiar with your husband's record-keeping system, determining his assets can be a time-consuming job. Don't hurry yourself. List them and return them to the box for safekeeping. You can always look again if something isn't clear to you.

Your next step as executrix is to bring the assets "under your control." As stated, this means that any bank accounts in your husband's name must be transferred to a new estate account in your name as executrix. The bank will tell you what they need in the way of documentation to make the switch of funds from his former accounts to "Mary S. Shaw, Executrix, Estate of Edward J. Shaw." You may also need to get an appraisal of the real properties he owned. "Real" here means land, with or without buildings on it. This includes property he owned separately, with you, or with anyone else. You will also need to know the current value of the house in which you live, assuming you own it, if the deed is in both your names. You will need an evaluation of any automobiles, jewelry, art collections, or other valuables. Probably the bank can be helpful here by suggesting the names of professional appraisers in various fields. Even if you are the sole beneficiary of the estate and the court will not require you to file an accounting of these assets, you will need this information in order to help prepare the estate's income tax return.

To make your inventory of the estate complete, values need to be assigned to the securities. This may be your first chance to discover how indispensable a pocket calculator can be unless you are a math whiz who never makes a mistake in your checkbook. They are cheap and sun or battery operated. When the battery is weak in a calculator you will know it, an advantage they have over tape recorders. Calculators are best worked with the eraser end of a lead pencil because that is smaller than your fingertip and won't slip off the keys. If you are hesitant about using one, ask any child over six to give you a quick course. You need a calculator to do the arithmetic that is involved. You will be a lot faster with the aid of this handy tool.

When you record the names that show on the face of each stock and bond certificate also record the number of shares or bonds owned. Next you need to get the value of these securities at the time of your husband's death. By far the easiest way to get this information is to ask the *Wall Street Journal* for the issue from the first business day following your husband's death. They are very obliging about such matters, and this is a lot simpler than digging it out of the library. Keep the paper for later when you have finished the chapters on investments, which explain how to read the financial pages, unless you already know. Another way to get information is to call your husband's stockbroker, if you know who he is. He can give you the amounts.

When you have the price of the stocks and bonds your husband held on the day in question, simply multiply the price by the number of shares of stock or the number of bonds. That will give you the value of each security on that date, and that is the figure the lawyer wants. Add the values of each holding, and you will have the figure *you* want—at least it's a beginning and a partial answer to how much money you will have.

Your husband probably kept a record somewhere of both his securities and yours, if you have any. Keeping these records is an important thing to do because, among other things, it lists how much was paid for what, when, and what the security paid out over the years. Try to find those records if you can. They are important for several reasons which will become clear later.

You may want to follow the bookkeeping method your husband set up. If so, set up a similar but new system in another place. A loose-leaf binder makes a convenient ledger because there will undoubtedly be changes made down the road. There is no one right way to keep this kind of information. The important thing is that it provide you with the data you need in a way that is easy for you to understand. You will also want to record the various values of the securities for later dates as time goes on, so leave some room for this. A later chapter covers this process in detail.

After you have assembled this considerable body of information, you will know the size of the gross amount of your husband's estate. But you still may not know the debts or taxes to be paid, if any, so you can't be sure yet what will be left over to distribute. If you feel a little dazed by all this, remember the attorney is there to help you every step of the way. That's what he is being paid to do; don't hesitate to call. Also, since his instructions to you are on tape, you don't have to belabor your memory or worry about forgetting them. Be thorough rather than quick, and make sure you understand what you are doing at each step before you go on to the next. You are building a solid foundation for your financial education when you do this.

As you gather the assets of the estate, you will be performing a second important function as executrix, that is, discovering the estate's legitimate debts. A legal notice in the classified section of a local paper notifies creditors to file their claims against the estate. The lawyer's office takes care of this advertisement. In California, your husband's creditors have four months from the date you become executrix to send in their bills. In all probability most of the bills have arrived. Put them in an appropriately marked file folder, and don't worry about them for the time being, except those for any private duty nurses. Pay them immediately from estate funds if you can, and keep a record of the payments in the claim file. Private nurses usually need the money right away. After your authority as executrix has been approved and you are sure that all the debts are valid, send copies of the bills to the attorney, who will forward them to the court. As soon as the court approves them, you can pay them from estate funds.

Even if you are the sole beneficiary of the estate, you must keep track of checks that come in made out to your husband. List incoming amounts on one page giving the date of the check, the source of the funds, the amount of the check and the reason for it. List expenses paid out on another page, giving the date, the amount, and the reason for the payment. You can endorse checks made out to him as executrix and deposit them into the estate's account.

Now for the third step. The attorney has explained that with his help, you are responsible for preparing the state or federal death tax returns, if any. These taxes are normally due nine months after death, and tax returns require a statement of the assets and a computation of what the deductions are, which the attorney will prepare. It may be necessary for you to sell some securities in order to raise the money for this payment. This is another reason the attorney needs the "numbers" from you—to do his part. Besides tax payments and the previously mentioned bills, other expenses are computed as well. Add up one-half the mortgage payments you have made since his death on the real estate you owned together, which will remain an estate responsibility as long as you own the property. One-half the real estate taxes and one-half the insurance on the house are also estate responsibilities, plus your commission as executrix, which is the same as the attorney's fee except for additional expenses he may have incurred. Once all these obligations of the estate are added up, you can subtract them from the asset total, and you will have an approximate total of what the estate will have left to pay out. The estate's participation in the major overhead for the house will continue until the estate is finally settled, and as mentioned above, this may be a good deal longer than nine months. What happens after that depends on the terms of the will.

Probably your attorney will have mentioned more than once that it is important to raise the cash to pay these estate expenses early. The money received from sale of stocks or bonds or whatever you decide to liquidate can be put into an insured, interest-bearing account. By doing this early, you avoid any panic selling at what could be a financially disadvantageous time closer to the date the payments are due. This is especially the case with real estate since it rarely moves quickly at the asking price. An insured account simply means one in a bank or thrift (another term for a savings and loan association) where accounts are insured up to $100,000 each. As mentioned in chapter three, these institutions offer many different sorts of insured accounts at varying rates of interest. Find out what you can on your own, then talk it over with the lawyer, who can tell you when you must have cash ready for payment. This will help you determine the kind of account you will want, as many have fixed time limits for maturity and a penalty for early withdrawal.

Liquidating assets, that is, exchanging assets for cash, may be new to you. Your main decision will be which of the various investments your husband made you will convert to cash. Several factors will influence this decision, and this is probably the time to seek the services of a competent professional in the investment field. In fact, you may find you require advice from people in several different fields, depending on the nature of the investments. If you have money tied up in real estate, oil wells, stocks, bonds, art, rare books, antique cars, or other collectibles, you will need good advice from several sources.

In addition to advice about the monetary worth of different components of the estate, you will be making decisions about your personal priorities. Some assets you may want to keep in their present form, and some you may want to get rid of because you don't care to be bothered with them or don't understand them. Perhaps some have increased in value and should be sold or kept for further gain. And there are always tax considerations. Finding out about these things can be an adventurous experience of discovery, and knowledgeable friends or the lawyer can probably suggest where to go for advice. One thing leads to another, and you will quickly become more comfortable as you gain knowledge. When ready, not before, make your decision—it is yours alone to make.

If you can find the people your husband did business with in these matters, by all means make an appointment to see them first of all. Organize your thoughts ahead of time and prepare a list of questions you want answered. Try not to prejudge whether or not these are questions you *should* ask. If a questions has come to your mind and the answer has not, by all means ask it. You have every reason to want the information and none whatever to be shy or hesitant about asking.

Another suggestion that might aid you in the process: in the interest of time and safety, make photo slides of any artworks or collected items, and write a detailed description of the things you can't photograph so that you can get accurate and specific advice. Be sure to take your tape recorder and tape each entire session you will have with appraisers, investment counselors, and any other professionals you call upon.

The federal death tax laws require that any liquidated assets be insured. Liquid assets include cash or funds instantly convertible to cash such as ordinary savings or checking accounts. Money market funds, though as liquid as a savings account, are not insured and therefore do not qualify. If Uncle Sam is due to get a bite, he wants to be sure he will get what is owed him. If anything has to be sold to meet the tax obligation, the proceeds may be reinvested only in government-insured instruments. They may not go back into the stock market or other non-insured ventures until the estate is settled and the money is yours to handle at your discretion. None of these restrictions apply to what you received from your husband's life insurance policies naming you as beneficiary. Those funds are not part of his estate and therefore not subject to probate.

Before you sell anything, you should get advice about the tax consequences of whatever you are thinking of doing before you actually do it. Purely in terms of taxes, it may make more sense to sell one thing as opposed to another. If the whole matter of taxes is beyond you, and such an esoteric matter as this is beyond most professionals outside the field, you will want to consult your husband's tax adviser. His name will be on the copy of last year's income tax return, right below where you signed with your husband. This person could be the best choice, because he is familiar with your situation. If your husband did his tax returns himself, you can ask friends or consult your ever-available attorney for suggestions about a reputable and able accountant.

It is worth exploring this matter in depth to find someone with whom you feel personally compatible. Especially at first, you will have a lot of dealings with the accountant until you have learned to file all the right receipts, keep records for tax purposes and make notations in your checkbook of what you spend money on that could be tax deductible. You will have to assemble figures for your accountant year after year as long as you live, as it is unlikely you will ever want to prepare your own tax returns. This paperwork all gets easier as you go along.

One former Internal Revenue Service (IRS) agent made the comment that returns prepared by professionals are less likely to be audited than those prepared by the taxpayer. An audit is a close examination of your return by the IRS to make sure everything is valid and in order. Some businesspersons enjoy the process of preparing their own returns, and they feel triumphant if their return stands as submitted after being audited. You are probably not in the mood for playing that game. However, take a close look at the various tax guidebooks that bloom along with the croucuses after the first of the year on almost all magazine stands. These manuals for getting through the tax maze are worth studying. You'll pick up a lot of information, some new and useful vocabulary, and perhaps even a few helpful hints that may have considerable benefit to you, such as turning extra space into a rental unit or something else that has tax advantages.

As mentioned earlier, accountant's fees are high, but they are also tax deductible. In addition to reducing the fees according to the amount of preliminary work you do yourself, this sort of paperwork is highly educational and will increase your self-confidence greatly as you master the process.

There is one more area of the estate settlement that warrants discussion. Several times in this chapter I made reference to assets held "in joint tenancy." This is something that deserves fuller attention in cases where the husband or wife (or both) has children by a previous marriage, a very common suitation these days. When the assets of a husband and wife are held as joint tenants, the children of the first to die may be seriously disadvantaged. This is true because property owned in joint tenancy automatically passes over to the survivor and is not governed by the terms of the deceased's will.

In other words, let's say your husband had children from a previous marriage. He felt he had provided for them by creating Trusts A and B in his will to convey his separate property and his half of whatever the two of you owned jointly to them upon your death. This was a common procedure prior to 1982. Any asset registered in "joint tenancy" bypasses the provisions of his will, and such assets automatically become yours beyond the control of the will. If they were registered instead by the phrase "tenants-in-common" or as community property, that would not be the case. This means then that your husband's assets registered in "joint tenancy" have become part of *your* estate and will be controlled by your will alone. In other words, when you die, these assets are totally yours to dispose of, and his children lost out or, at best, are subject to your decisions about his wishes as you understood them. Under community property or tenants-in-common, however, the husband can direct in his will that when his wife dies his half of the community property goes to his children by the previous marriage.

Upon passage of the Economic Recovery Tax Act (ERTA), some changes were made that, among other things, provide protection for children by a previous marriage. It is the QTIP trust (Qualified *Terminable* Interest Property), and the key word is "terminable." Under its provision, the surviving spouse receives income only, for life, which must be paid out at least annually. The trust assets cannot be disposed of by the survivor's will, but are controlled by the will of the decedent upon the death of the survivor.

Another significant change enacted by ERTA is the unlimited marital deduction. In other words, to quote Louis G.

Russell III, noted CPA from Alabama, "The changes brought about provide that unlimited amounts of property. . . . can be transferred between spouses without estate or gift tax." Only women whose husbands died prior to the passage of ERTA can appreciate the financial burden it removed.

The QTIP election by the executor of a will drawn up prior to 1982, when the act became effective, is available as an option to the executor for fifteen months, to decide whether or not to elect the marital deduction treatment for the QTIP. It has considerable tax benefits.

For some reason, even in these days of very high rates of divorce and remarriage, the significant difference between community property and joint tenancy has not been given much attention. Joint tenancy seems to be a common way for stockbrokers to register securities, perhaps assuming that the client understands what it means, though often the client does not.

To illustrate this dilemma in more detail, assume that each of you has children from previous marriages. Each of your wills created the two trusts, Trust A and Trust B. After the first of you dies, in this case the husband, the estate is settled and a trustee is required to be appointed to administer the trusts. The trustee divides the trust estate, which consists of everything the deceased owned as separate property or community property, in two parts, A and B. Trust A consists of the marital deduction, which by 1987 will gradually increase to $600,000. (Before the 1981 Tax Act it was $175,625.) Trust B consists of everything left over. The quotation from an actual will shows how these trusts operate.

If my wife survives me the Trustee shall set aside as Trust A that amount that will equal the maximum marital deduction allowable in my estate for federal estate tax purposes, reduced by the federal estate tax values of all other property interests that pass or have passed to my wife, under the provisions of this will or otherwise. . . .

All of the balance of the trust estate . . . shall be set aside by the trustee as Trust B.

The trustee shall pay to my wife during her lifetime, the entire net income of both Trusts A and B.

On the death of my wife, the Trustee shall distribute the balance remaining to Trust A to one or more persons, including her own estate, as my wife shall appoint by a will.

Any of Trust A not effectively appointed by my wife shall be added to Trust B to follow the disposition as hereafter provided.

This passage from a will has been greatly abbreviated, but I believe the points are clear.

It is a common practice for husbands and wives to have reciprocal wills in which each has a life interest in the estate of the other. And, if there are children from previous marriages, on the death of the survivor the husband's children would inherit what was set up by prior arrangement of his estate and the wife's children receive what was subject to the control of her will. This seems a simple concept, but any such arrangements are destroyed by the provision of joint tenancy of assets.

Financial advisors have little interest in where the money goes after someone dies, but parents have a great interest in this issue. Also, financial advisors rarely know the marital history of a client, but the attorney who draws up the will does. Therefore, the attorney should ask how jointly owned property is registered and explain the consequences of the choices while there is time to reregister the joint assets in accordance with the actual wishes of the people involved.

If a situation as described here does happen, only the surviving stepparent can rectify the damage when he or she draws up a new will. It can be corrected on a ratio basis by figuring out the relationship of the assets of the deceased to the survivor's total holdings. That is, the ratio of his separate property plus one-half of the jointly owned assets to the wife's separate holdings plus one-half of the jointly owned assets. The proportion of the survivor's estate can then be bequeathed to the stepchildren in a new will.

This may sound very confusing. Should the situation described apply to you, go over it with your attorney—that is, if you feel strongly about carrying out the intent of your husband's will. You will need to have a new will, in any case. If you have children by a previous marriage and imagine a reverse in the sequence of your deaths, you will get a clearer picture of how your children by an earlier marriage might have been deprived of a portion of what you thought would be willed to them in your estate.

To return, having gathered the assets of the estate, taken them under your control, paid the estate's debts and taxes if any, you are about to wind up the job of being executrix. You prepare a complete accounting, showing all the money that has come into the estate since your husband's death and where it came from, all the money paid out from the estate and what for, and all the assets that remain on hand. Even if you are the sole beneficiary of the estate, in which case the court will not require you to file an accounting, this information will be needed to prepare the estate's income tax returns.

The attorney next presents a petition for final distribution to the court. Three or four weeks after this, another hearing will be set, which you need not attend. Then following this hearing, you will distribute the assets of the estate to the people named in the will if there are any besides yourself. You will pay the attorney his fees and yourself your executrix's commissions, and your duties as executrix will be over.

Though the accounting and payment of taxes, if any, had to

be completed in nine months, it may be longer than that before the distribution is made and you and the attorney are paid. However, the most difficult work is done. You'll find it hard to believe how much you have learned during this process until you replay the tapes from some of your first sessions in the lawyer's office. Words that once sounded foreign have become part of your everyday vocabulary. Arduous and time consuming as this has been, you have added immensely to your knowledge of legal and financial matters, and you will be able to draw upon this storehouse of information to your benefit as long as you live.

You have learned something of the difference between stocks and bonds from holding the certificates in your hands and reading them, and you will learn a lot more about the differences in the chapters that follow. You know where your money will come from, and you have probably begun to take an interest in taxes, the cost of owning a home, and the various ways to invest money. In addition, you now understand most of the terms the lawyer uses when he slips into legal jargon—phrases like "interest in community property," where interest means participation, and "marital deduction," which is what the federal estate tax allows you to set aside for yourself from your husband's estate before it is totaled up for the IRS. You know that net is what is left of the estate after all taxes, expenses, and deductions are subtracted from the gross, which is the total value of the estate before it was reduced by these obligations. You have gained some new interpersonal skills and are no longer over-awed at the knowledge displayed by the specialized professionals you have dealt with. You respect them now and feel more comfortable working with them. You have mastered several useful tools in the process, as well; you know how to make use of a copying machine, a tape-recorder, and a calculator. You have also set up a record-keeping system and organized a complex set of files. Not bad for a woman who just a while ago was in such a state of abysmal depression she didn't know what to do nor how to begin to settle her overwhelming practical problems.

Don't consider settling his estate a waste of time, thinking that you will never again need the specialized knowledge you acquired. Some of your friends will one day be in the same boat you were, and you will be able to help calm their fears and uncertainties by explaining the process to them. In this case, ignorance is the cause of fear, and experience allays it. Discharging this responsibility is a big step toward regaining a sense of equilibrium.

CHAPTER FIVE

Your Physical and Financial Balance

While you are proceeding with your husband's estate, time passes and life goes on. You begin to get the hang of what you are doing and see the need to keep good records. Perhaps the knot of anxiety—like a lump of cold dough in the pit of your stomach—has begun to dissipate and you feel a bit more relaxed, a trifle less afraid of trying to manage on your own.

In fact, you are doing just that—managing alone. The money from the insurance policies has arrived and is in a savings account temporarily. Your initial fear that you would be alone all the time has evaporated—you may even have a problem because you aren't alone enough. Friends are very kind, or it seems to you they are just being kind. You still can't admit to yourself that they like to see you and that it wasn't just your husband they wanted to see in the past. Your friends, in fact, can wear you out with dinner invitations if you accept them all out of a concern that you will be forgotten if you don't.

Fatigue is pervasive at a time like this. If you used to think of yourself as a healthy woman, perhaps now you are troubled about your low energy level. Stress reveals itself in insidious ways that should not be ignored. Temporary memory lapse is one you know about, but you can laugh about this a bit now since you have developed methods of coping with it. But perhaps you have some other new physical problems or you aren't sleeping well. If these stress symptoms worry you, this is a good time to make an appointment with your doctor for a physical check-up. As with any matter of importance you plan to discuss with a professional who will bill you for time spent, make a list before you go of what you want to talk with your physician about. Note your symptoms, such as sleep loss, split fingernails, lack of energy, weakness, shakiness.

You might also take note of your eating habits, how and what you are doing for nutrition. Are you snacking a lot because you don't feel like cooking just for yourself? If you never liked to cook before, doubtless you've nearly taken a vacation from it, which is all right so long as your intake of food is balanced. Balanced, according to Lelord Kordel who wrote *Eat and Grow Younger,* means paying attention to four categories of food: proteins, carbohydrates (sugars and starches), fats, and water. He describes protein as the basic raw material of life stored only in living tissue and in places where it is essential for the development of new life—the embryo of eggs, milk needed to nourish the young, and the seeds of plants. Thus protein is found in meat, fowl and fish, eggs and milk, cereal and seed grains, and nuts and legumes. If the word legumes bothers you, it is often used in its plural form to mean vegetables in general. Dr. Kordel lists what he considers to be a proper balanced daily food guideline.

- 1 serving of meat, poultry or fish
- 1 egg
- 3 slices whole grain bread

- 1 pint fresh skim milk, buttermilk, cottage cheese or other cheeses
- 1 serving of dried lentils, whole grain or seed cereal
- 1 serving of cooked vegetable
- 1 green salad
- 1 serving fresh or cooked fruit

This list gives you a working idea of what balanced eating means. In short, this is not the time to live on chocolate milkshakes or bread and jelly sandwiches. You know that, of course, but you may not have been paying attention to your diet. You can eat quite simply, do little or no cooking—certainly no elaborate cooking—and still eat very well as far as your body's needs go. If variety is not something you care about now, work out a basic week's menu and follow it until you get some interest and energy for getting back to cookbooks. That way you can save yourself the trouble of thinking much about food, yet still be sure you are taking good care of your nutritional needs.

Most doctors of the traditional school don't enthuse over vitamins, saying you can get all you need if you eat a balanced diet. But vitamins shouldn't be rejected too hastily. For example, a woman broke out with herpes zoster, called shingles, on the side of her face and in her hair a short time before a wedding was to be held at her house. She went to her doctor, who sympathized but told her there was no treatment for it, that it would probably be gone in a few months, but she might be left with some scars. However, his nurse walked down the hall with her to the waiting room and suggested she get some vitamin E capsules, "Cut them in half and smear the oil on the sores." Later, the doctor was amazed to learn that following this treatment, the symptoms disappeared within three weeks leaving no scars at all. The moral is, if you are taking vitamins, this is no time to stop. And if you have not been in the habit of taking them, ask among your friends about their experiences. Vitamins might help and certainly can't do you any harm.

Among other queries, your physician is likely to ask how much exercise you get. Probably not nearly enough. Very likely he or she will suggest walking a certain distance each day or doing some other exercise regularly. If that isn't appealing to you or you need something extra to get started, think about giving yourself a special treat and inquire about a spa—sometimes called a "fat farm" though the people who go there are seldom much overweight. Spa programs are not cheap, but a week of doing as much as you can to get in shape at one of these places will make you feel more physically fit than you have for years. If a friend goes with you, so much the better. When your body is limber and supple, there is little question that your head and your heart will feel better too.

Aside from taking care of your physical self to give yourself a boost, you can improve your state of mind by finding out how much it is costing you to live as you now do. This essential information will enable you to make intelligent decisions farther down the road. To help you make an accurate record, you might like to buy a booklet available in stationery stores called *Ekonomik Home Treasurer.* If you can't find it, write to Ekonomik Systems, P.O. Box 11413, Tacoma, Washington 98411. This booklet shows you how to keep track of your expenses by category, such as personal, automobile, housing, charities/church, insurance, medical-dental-drugs, utilities, clothing, food, recreation, and taxes. It is well-arranged and seems easier to use than a system one might create from scratch. Most stationery stores carry some form of budget record like this.

After six months of keeping this kind of record, you will have a clear and exact picture of your lifestyle. Just transfer your checkbook notations into the category-type of record, and you will get a picture of where your money goes that nothing else can provide. If the result of breaking down your living expenses and then adding them all up gives you a nasty shock, don't panic. This is the most common reaction. Look at your records again, and try to pick out the non-recurring expenses that had to do with your husband's death; perhaps a huge telephone bill, expenses for out-of-town relatives, and so on. There will be other items such as subscriptions, donations, memberships that you have renewed without thinking because they were part of the way you used to live together. Perhaps your husband owned a boat that also involves expenses and a membership at the yacht club, or you have a second home on which the bills keep coming in. You may not want to keep these things now, or you may want to make them money-producers by renting them out until you can come to a final decision. Possibly you and your husband were very generous to your young who always seemed short of funds, and you could easily spare it. Without thinking, you made your recent gifts to them as generous as ever, more than feels comfortable in your new circumstances.

This is still too early to make major decisions on what expenses are appropriate for you now, but it isn't too soon to begin thinking about them. Even if you haven't gone through your husband's checkbook yet and haven't discovered how much of the family income ceased upon his death, you may realize from your records that you have less money coming in than you have spent.

You are not yet in a position to decide what changes you want to make because you simply don't know. Probably the best thing is to accommodate yourself to the situation as best you can—to take care of yourself physically and keep studying the information you have and organize it so that you understand it.

In terms of income, one of the changes could be Social Security benefits. If your husband was receiving them, the checks have stopped coming because the lawyer reminded you to notify the local Social Security office of his death. Without trying to unravel the complexities of the system and how it works, you probably qualify as a recipient. That was part of the purpose toward which he paid increasing sums during his working life; a program of enforced savings during the earning years for the benefit of a steady, if fairly modest, income upon retirement. By all means go to the Social Security office nearest you, taking his social security card and your own with you, and state your case. As a rule, the personnel there are understanding and patient. Most of their time is spent with people like you who have no idea what is in store. You will probably become the charge of a particular worker who will give you his or her telephone number at work and urge that you communicate by phone as much as possible. You will also be asked for various sorts of documentation and after a while the records will get straightened out and the checks will start to come in.

Your next step in coming to terms with your financial balance is to get some idea of what the return is on the investments your husband made: what they pay and what percent of return you are getting for the amounts they represent. Your income from investments will be clearer to you if, as dividend or interest checks come in, you set up a chart for them. This way you will know when to expect the next payment from the same source. One useful way to do this is shown on the chart "Annual Projection, Anticipated Income—Securities." (See page 65.)

On a standard 8½x11 piece of lined paper, make seven vertical columns with a ruler. The lines should be about half an inch apart, starting from the right-hand side. This leaves the room you will need on the left side of the page. Beginning at the top of the first column on the left, label the columns Jan/Jul, Feb/Aug, Mar/Sept, Apr/Oct, May/Nov, and Jun/Dec. Dividends are paid quarterly, so each will show up twice in the chart; bonds pay interest semiannually, so that payment will show up only once. When all the payments are listed, you add them up for a six-month total. Then double this figure for the total income you can expect from the securities for a year. However, that is getting ahead of where you are right now.

As the checks come in, list the company that issued each of them on the left of the page and add the *date* and the month it arrived. Enter the amount of the check in the column to the right under the proper paired months. If, for example, a check came in from Pennwalt Corporation for $330 on May 5, put 5 after the name of the company, Pennwalt, and the amount in the proper monthly columns, $330 in the columns headed May/Nov, and Feb/Aug. Then you know when to expect the next check. Remember, this applies only to *dividend* checks. *Interest* checks derived from bonds should be entered only once, since our sheet runs for six months, and they come in only twice a year. The check itself will tell you whether it is an interest or dividend check.

Using a system of this sort, plus whatever comes in monthly listed here as "other," you can estimate what your income for the next year is likely to be. This is more important to your peace of mind right now than knowing the total value of everything you will own when the estate is finally settled. Once you know what your yearly income is from investments, you may want to go further and find out

Income Projection 1986
Common Stocks & Conv. Debentures Only

STOCKS	Dividend date	No. Shares	Jan July	Feb Aug	Mar Sept	Apr Oct	May Nov	June Dec	6 mos
Amer. Home Pro.	2	600			435			435	870
Amoco	11	500			412			412	824
A.T. Cross. (ASE)	17	1000		360			360		720
Ft. Howard *S*	28	1000	259			259			518
Heinz *S*	12	1800	360			360			720
IBM	10	328	360			360			720
Merck	2	300	270			270			540
M.M.M	12	400	350			350			1080
Pitney-Bowes	12	1000			300			300	600
Rubberm'd *S*	3	800			96			96	192
Wisc. E.&.P.	3	1350			837			837	1672
DEBENTURES									
25 M. K Mart	6's, '99	16	750						750
30 M. Lomas & Nett.	9's, '10	15		1462					1462
			2349	1822	2080	1599	360	2080	10,668

6 mos. × 2 = annual 20,583

S = Split
ASF = American Stock Exchange

more about the sources of this money. Are the companies really contemporary in this changing world? Would they be good places to invest more money?

By now you have received in the mail quarterly or annual reports of the companies your family funds are invested with. These sometimes elegant reports are full of encouraging words, but the figures tell you a great deal more about each company. Merrill Lynch, Pierce, Fenner and Smith once issued a fine little handbook called *How to Read a Financial*

Report. It was first issued in 1962, but it deals with timeless facts that don't go out-of-date, and it is still available and helpful.

What follows is a very simplified explanation of what the annual reports are all about. I have used a Merck & Company balance sheet and earnings statement. A *balance sheet* is like a photograph of a company's financial condition. It tells where the company stood at a particular point in time—usually the end of the current calendar or fiscal year or other periods described, and for the same time periods a year earlier, and perhaps more previous years are included.

Under assets are listed cash and short-term investments, which usually means stocks, bonds, and government securities. Next is accounts receivable, the money owed the company by its customers. Inventories represent whatever the company sells while it is still in the company's possession. Prepaid expenses and taxes are self-explanatory. Property, plant and equipment seem clear; the depreciation item refers to everything tangible except land, which does not depreciate. Depreciation is a reduction in value, for tax accounting purposes, caused by the passage of time and other factors; it is a financial recognition that items wear out over an extended period. Investments and other assets usually reflect ownership of a subsidiary company by the parent company, the one issuing the report.

The liability side represents debts owed. Current liabilities are the company's obligations to its regular suppliers; wages and salaries to personnel, attorney's fees, pensions, insurance premiums, and so on. Taxes are listed separately, as are dividends due to be paid stockholders, and loans payable are presumably due to banks.

Long-term debt refers to obligations more than a year away from settlement date. Other liabilities can be almost anything the company owes to another entity, and minority interest in

Consolidated Balance Sheet

Merck & Co., Inc. and Subsidiaries — December 31

Assets	1983	1982
Current Assets		
Cash and short-term investments	$ 370,744,000	$ 313,242,000
Accounts receivable	709,420,000	645,290,000
Inventories	566,724,000	628,615,000
Prepaid expenses and taxes	85,956,000	97,999,000
Total current assets	1,732,844,000	1,685,146,000
Property, Plant, and Equipment, at cost		
Land	64,603,000	42,822,000
Buildings	713,416,000	654,640,000
Machinery, equipment, and office furnishings	1,637,992,000	1,509,540,000
Construction in progress	244,607,000	189,798,000
	2,660,618,000	2,396,800,000
Less allowance for depreciation	945,411,000	839,310,000
	1,715,207,000	1,557,490,000
Investments Maturing Beyond One Year, at cost which approximates market	92,406,000	124,566,000
Other Assets	674,241,000	288,179,000
	$4,214,698,000	$3,655,381,000

Liabilities and Stockholders' Equity		
Current Liabilities		
Accounts payable and accrued liabilities	$ 508,459,000	$ 400,214,000
Income taxes payable	63,321,000	108,083,000
Dividends payable	55,405,000	51,726,000
Loans payable	370,770,000	264,754,000
Total current liabilities	997,955,000	824,777,000
Long-Term Debt	385,468,000	337,293,000
Deferred Income Taxes and Other Liabilities	373,356,000	265,610,000
Minority Interests in Foreign Subsidiaries	23,306,000	23,713,000

Consolidated Balance Sheet (cont.)

Merck & Co., Inc. and Subsidiaries — December 31

Stockholders' Equity		
Common stock	2,109,000	2,109,000
Other paid-in capital	154,776,000	155,395,000
Deferred compensation payable in common stock	24,696,000	23,838,000
Retained earnings	2,407,656,000	2,176,155,000
	2,589,237,000	2,357,497,000
Less treasury stock, at cost	154,624,000	153,509,000
Total stockholders' equity	2,434,613,000	2,203,988,000
	$4,214,698,000	$3,655,381,000

Consolidated Statement of Income

Merck & Co., Inc. and Subsidiaries — Years Ended December 31

	1983	1982	1981
Sales	$3,246,139,000	$3,063,017,000	$2,929,455,000
Costs and Expenses			
Materials and production costs	1,263,369,000	1,222,228,000	1,229,298,000
Marketing, administrative, and research expenses	1,261,088,000	1,212,387,000	1,111,460,000
Interest (net) and other	29,369,000	29,886,000	2,433,000
	2,553,826,000	2,464,501,000	2,343,191,000
Income Before Taxes	692,313,000	598,516,000	586,264,000
Taxes on Income	245,100,000	185,500,000	187,600,000
Minority Interests	(3,642,000)	(2,121,000)	399,000
Net Income	$ 450,855,000	$ 415,137,000	$ 398,265,000
Earnings Per Share of Common Stock	$6.10	$5.61	$5.36

Supplementary Income Statement Information	1983	1982	1981
Research and development expenses	$ 356,045,000	$ 320,156,000	$ 274,168,000
Advertising expenses	97,410,000	86,351,000	80,931,000
Repairs, alterations, and maintenance	92,592,000	95,321,000	95,697,000
Taxes, other than income, principally payroll taxes	94,490,000	95,334,000	88,441,000
Interest expense, net of amounts capitalized	74,842,000	51,599,000	35,286,000
Interest income	42,635,000	35,422,000	40,047,000

foreign subsidiaries means just what it says. Stockholders' equity is the difference between the total assets of the business and its total liabilities. In other words, the net worth of the business. The process here is basically the same as you used to assess your husband's estate—the assets or gross holdings, the debts, and the difference between them is the net—what the estate had to distribute, or in this case, the company.

Next is the income statement, also known as the statement of profit and loss, the earnings report, or, in Merck's case, statements of consolidated income. The balance sheet gives a picture of the financial soundness of a company on the date it was issued. The income statement gives a lot of signals about the future. The sales figures are given, and the consolidated costs of the sales are subtracted, which leaves the income-before-taxes figure. But taxes have to be paid, so that figure is subtracted, too, which—after one more subtraction for minority interests (subsidiary companies)—leaves the net income. That is the amount available for dividends to the stockholders and for reinvesting in the business. Depending on the decisions made by the board of directors, the pie will be split according to some plan. This means that the earnings per share of common stock is not the same as the dividend your shares will earn for you. It is just a way of measuring the overall profits from which the dividends are paid.

The performance of a company over a period of years is much more important than what is contained in the annual report of any one year. This is an essential fact to keep in mind.

When you start talking to people in the investment world, you will hear a lot about the P/E ratio of a company. This is not a physical education program for company managers. It is the price/earnings ratio, and it refers to the relationship between the earnings per share of a company's stock and the current price per share. For example, if a stock is selling at $50 and is earning $2 per share, its price/earnings ratio is twenty-five. That means the stock is selling at twenty-five times earnings—rather high. A stock might be considered a good buy at a P/E of five or ten, depending on the economic climate. P/Es will be discussed in relation to specific stocks and the health of a general field of an industry in a later chapter.

The thing to keep in mind about annual reports is that they are published by the company and so are self-serving. Discussing the prose used in some annual reports, Thomas Petzinger, Jr., wrote in the *Wall Street Journal,* "Executive double-talk springs from a special vocabulary. It favors the passive voice, allowing troubled firms to depict themselves as victims of sinister forces beyond their control. Mirro Corporation says it had a 'milestone year!' That year it lost $2.1 million and is planning the sale of more than half the company." He comments further that some investment advisers regard unclear writings as a corporate cover-up. "The amount of pontificating a company does varies in direct proportion to how screwed up it is," says David Bartlett, research director at an investment firm.

A widow's need for financial knowledge is no different from anyone else's; this is the firmly held conviction of Kit Cole, founder of the Cole Financial Group, an investment firm. She gives courses on personal money management. "There are a lot of corporate executives who are no wiser about running their own affairs than their widows will be," she says. "It doesn't necessarily translate that just because they are good at a certain business, their investment judgments are sound." Cole believes that everyone should make a start at managing their own finances and that the best way to do this is to put down on paper what is currently going on in their lives. With this as a start, the next step is to build up their objectives.

"People often don't know how to deal with their lives, sometimes for long-standing ethical reasons. A lot of things besides lack of financial information enter in, one of which is the Puritan Ethic dictum that you don't think about your needs or your wants but you live within your income—whatever that means," she commented.

"It is equally valid to look at your resources and then decide what you want to do and make your resources work for you toward that end, instead of being at the mercy of your resources. If your resources are bringing you in an amount that only permits you to live very modestly but you surmise that a better income is available if some changes were made, you will want to find out what your investment alternatives are—people typically don't use such an approach."

Discussing the usual confusion in people's minds, Cole said they come to her firm for financial counseling on a fee-per-hour basis, and when asked what they want and what is important to them, they very often reply that they don't know and they haven't really thought about it. And the reason they haven't thought about what they want is because they feel they can't afford it. "How do they know they can't afford it if they don't know where they are?'' Cole queries. ''We make suppositions like that all our lives, and they become self-fulfilling prophecies just because we believe in them. At our firm, we try to give the fundamentals and get people to look at their finances in a more positive fashion than they have in the past. We tell them what records they have to keep and how to set up their files.''

Speaking specifically about widows, she says, ''You have to learn a whole new mode of thinking when you are in a bereaved state.'' *Being accountable for yourself*—most of us didn't grow up with that concept. Instead we grew up expecting someone else to take care of us. As it turns out, a lot of the concepts we have believed and lived with are not realistic for today's world.

In the Hospice program, where she gives lectures on money management, Kit Cole says, ''We talk about what you need to know to take charge of your financial affairs. When you realize that all financial decisions are made with an eye to maintaining your lifestyle, you have to know what your lifestyle is or what it costs you every year to live. Before you start investing in stocks and bonds, you have to go back over a twelve-month period and see, on a month-by-month basis, where you are spending your money. Mortgage payments, insurance, taxes, it's only a matter of putting it down on paper, not making moral judgments about it.'' She suggests taking your check register as a good accounting of how you spend your money. (If you're paying cash, stop doing it. You should be writing checks because they give you a way of evaluating what you are doing.) You need to have this record.

Once you know your income and its sources and your basic living expenses, you can begin to consider options or changes, though it must be stressed that this is purely a mental process at this point—no big decisions yet.

A major change in your lifestyle that will come up is when

you consider selling your home. You may have thought of it yourself, or it may even have been suggested by an insensitive real estate person looking for a listing. There is a widow's rule of thumb in response to that—make no major changes in the way you live for at least the first year you live alone.

Some women act in haste because their home is so full of memories they can't bear the thought of staying there. But if you move away in that frame of mind, you are giving in to the tempting hope of escape from the pain of grief. This hope is not based on reality and will only complicate your recovery more. This is not to say that selling the place is a bad idea. If it is too big or a burden to you financially or you find another spot you would really prefer to live, selling your home eventually may be your best choice—when you have sorted out your priorities.

If you aren't convinced that escape is impossible, take a trip, try a cruise, visit some friends in a far-off place and see if it helps you. That's a much less complicated venture than selling your home. If you do feel better away than at home beyond being temporarily relieved of the chores, decisions, and paperwork involved in our new status, then perhaps you will conclude moving is the thing you want to do. But make the step slowly and carefully because you are convinced it is the only way you will ever be able to build a new life for yourself. After all, right now you are deeply involved in a process of becoming *unmarried* and that in itself is a monumental change.

To many who flee to the carefree life afloat, or some shoreside equivalent, the distress caused by seeing so many *couples* having a good time is worse than being at home alone. There seems an unremitting demand on you in such an environment to be sociable, pleasant, and give the appearance of having a good time.

Instead of finding such a trip restful and restorative, you could find it exhausting, trying to be two people at once. At some point you may indeed become a "merry widow," but the healing process has just begun and it is slow; very probably you aren't there yet. You may make an effort to be conversational with fellow travelers and admit to one or two people that your husband died recently. They will probably murmur sympathetic words and drop the matter, making you feel more alone than ever. People who don't know you well aren't the least interested in hearing about death and sorrow while on a vacation trip designed to get them away from mundane unpleasantness, never mind devastating loss. At home, you don't need to keep up any appearances or put on a false front when you might just feel like crying. It's probably a better idea to save the money and go later on, when your emotional state is more reliable.

Beyond the idea of selling the house and moving into another place with fewer responsibilities, you might also think about moving away from where you now live altogether, to live with or nearer your children and perhaps grandchildren. If your relationship with your child or children is a good one, they will probably bring the question up and offer to make whatever rearrangements in their own living habits it would take to accommodate you properly.

Children are often moved by great generosity at a time like this and are quite sincere in their invitation—but think this one over very carefully, too, and postpone making any decision. The longer you think about it, the more clearly and dispassionately you can assess any warning flags that go up. For example, what if the young had to move away for personal business reasons after you got there? Would you want to be entirely dependent on the next generation for your social life, at least for the time it would take you to establish your own? Establishing a whole new social life is not an easy thing to do at any time, and it is harder now. Moving in with them would almost certainly diminish your sense of independence, which is something you need to strengthen right now in order to feel competent and at peace with yourself. Make a visit, by all means, but stall a long time before you make such a permanent move.

The same sort of considerations, in general, apply to moving to a retirement residence or adult community by yourself. Some of them are delightful to the eye, and they do offer almost total security, if that has become a need. Moreover, they have the attraction of providing companionship with others in the same fix.

Probably a decision like this comes down to the sort of person you are and your ability to adjust to a solitary life. If you are convivial, feel better with many people around—with a string of new relationships, new activities, and new surroundings—and don't think you might be leaving too much behind, adult communities have a lot to offer.

Another possibility, depending on your temperament, is to rent out a part of your house to a suitable tenant, if your house is designed so that you can do this. Perhaps you could remodel part of it into a small, self-contained apartment or just a room and a bath. Sharing the kitchen can be a problem if you rent a room; you might be willing to have a tenant prepare his or her breakfast there and no other meals. On the other hand, you might so crave companionship, that the idea of having *someone* come home for dinner is a happy thought. There are endless variations on this possibility. You can probably work one out to suit your own preferences. True, some communities frown on such departures from the single-family dwelling if that is what you have, but in these days of insufficient housing and other pressures, formerly rigid zoning standards are changing.

In addition to any social benefits, having someone else in

the house has some modest financial rewards. You can attribute the overhead of the place to the rental unit on a proportional basis. For instance, if the unit equals one-eighth of your total floor space, you can deduct a similar proportion of the heating bill, water bill, property tax, and maintenance costs on your income tax return. This can balance the income you get from the rental unit. Talk it over with your tax accountant—it may turn out that you can deduct the entire expense from the tenant's rent. This way, the income not only doesn't boost your taxable income, it deducts from the overhead expense what would not otherwise produce any tax benefits because the expense of maintaining your own home is not deductible, nor is the value of the home depreciable—as rental properties are.

Eventually you will recover from this diminished state, but while this gradual process is taking place, you have many things to consider: where you live, where your friends are, where your children are if you have any, and which relationships will play the largest role for you in the years ahead. You may resentfully think that life was supposed to be sung as a duet, but as you achieve piece of mind by learning where you stand financially, how to manage your money with confidence, and what your personal options are, you will find that you can render a pretty satisfactory solo—perhaps a little squeaky at first—but finally in full throat.

Suit your inclinations. For quite a while your daily activities may be dictated by what arrives in the mail. As mentioned earlier, it is conducive to a sense of order in your life if you process as much of the mail as possible the day it arrives. Checks floating around with other papers on your desk have a way of getting misplaced and it takes a long time to replace one. Bills do not diminish in size when not attended to; they can even get quite a bit bigger. Develop the habit of paying bills on arrival. That way when your bank statement comes in, you can reconcile it with your checkbook and see your true state of solvency without subtracting a lot of outstanding checks. This works best if your bills are paid at least ten days before the statement is due to arrive. Banks, being banks, have a well-established routine; once you note the date the statement arrives, you can expect it to come in on the same date the next month and probably for years to come.

If you have always had problems balancing your checkbook, now is the time in your life to recognize that this particular trait needs immediate attention. There's nothing to be ashamed about because you and your checkbook always seem to be at odds or because you and the bank are never close to agreement. But it can and must be corrected, and the bank will help. Usually a woman with a sympathetic expression occupies at least one desk in your bank; ask her who to talk to about your problem. When you are sitting across from the right person, produce your checkbook, the previous month's statement, and the cancelled checks that came with it. She will help you clear up the errors, and you will learn a different way of dealing with your checks that should eliminate at least one source of monthly exasperation. You may feel more comfortable about your ability to follow the bank personnel's suggestions if you have them on tape; by all means bring your tape recorder along, and later replay the tape until you have all the steps clearly in mind. In a sense, the tape recorder is a substitute for a textbook of procedures in this and other situations you encounter that give you trouble. If you now make a habit of carrying loose blank checks in your wallet instead of your checkbook, break the habit. It only causes confusion because those checks often don't get recorded, and the imbalance with your statement is likely to remain a mystery, requiring a lot of extra paperwork.

As for those new automatic tellers, a simple way to record those withdrawals is to do it with some symbol in your checkbook before you leave the house to use the machine. For some reason, many people are skittish about using automatic tellers. These machines are almost always quicker than drive-up windows where so many people seem to engage in numerous and complex transactions while cars line up behind them. If you don't understand how to use the automatic teller, which the bank installed at considerable expense (one figure was $80,000 each), ask someone using it to show you how. Most people are glad to play teacher if they aren't in a rush. Getting used to automatic tellers is something like getting used to self-service gasoline pumps. Once you catch on, there's nothing to it. The automatic teller liberates you from regular banking hours. You can pull out those nice, crisp twenties at 6 a.m. on your way to the airport, having forgotten to get cash the day before, and you can make deposits any time in the night depository. Banks have come quite a way to make things convenient for the absent-minded. Just don't forget to enter your transactions in your check register, or you and the bank will be more at odds than ever.

While you are concerned with learning the ins and outs of your cash flow, you might get interested in putting some money aside. Saving money can be an engaging project, offering as it does its own reward. Some widows, unaccustomed to having so much money under their control for the first time in their lives, spend it with abandon as though it poured out of a bottomless reservoir. They are the ones the insurance companies mention as having lost (or spent) most of what they acquired upon their husband's death in an alarmingly short time. You are not one of those or you would not be reading this book.

What you now have—with your husband no longer here—is probably all you will ever get by inheritance, assuming that your parents are also deceased. You realize this and know it is up to you to handle this money wisely. You are most likely looking to the years ahead as a period when you hope to increase the value of your capital assets and your income along with them. This is as it should be. The next three chapters discuss various ways in which money can be successfully managed. Through an understanding of how the investment world operates, you can gain confidence in yourself and your future.

CHAPTER SIX

Welcome to Wall Street

J. P. Morgan, the legendary financier, was once asked wha he thought the stock market would do. His simple answe was, "It will fluctuate." Adam Amith, a carefully chose pseudonym, writes in *The Money Game*, "The first rule o making money is not to lose it." Neither statement is exactl a revelation about the world of high finance, but Smit concedes the implication that "The professional investors ar smarter than the small investor is not true—they are no smarter, they merely have more information."

For you, investing is not a money game; it is no sort o *game* at all. Managing your capital is probably the mos serious matter you ever dealt with, after deciding who yo were going to marry.

Normally, most women haven't been given any preparatio for getting into financial markets. If you don't know th difference between a stock and a bond, or between dividend and interest, you belong to a sizeable majority. But read o and these apparent mysteries will come clear.

One basic problem is that the investment world has a language of its own. For example, dividends and interest are not discussed as income, a word you would readily understand. A lot of terms will be defined and their differences explained in these chapters. After you have started to become familiar with them, you should develop more confidence about asking questions to learn whatever it is you don't know or understand. The person to ask is whoever is helping you manage your financial affairs. Even more important, you will develop the ability to evaluate intelligently the answers you get. Is what you are hearing useful or meaningful to you? Are the people you are talking with misunderstanding what you are saying or not hearing you correctly? Do your consultants understand your situation thoroughly? The important thing is to know what questions to ask, know whether the answers are intelligent, and know what the answers mean.

A good way to introduce yourself to the world of investments in the stock or bond markets is to visit the office of a large firm of stockbrokers. If you have never been inside one, treat yourself to a remarkable experience by dropping in at Merrill Lynch, Pierce, Fenner and Smith in any big city. That firm is the biggest retailer of stocks and bonds in the country; they have offices almost everywhere.

A brokerage firm is an interesting place to look around, but it's not everybody's idea of an office. Imagine a room the size of a basketball court sectioned off into little cubicles perhaps six feet by six feet, each with a desk, two chairs and the indispensable telephone, plus books and papers on every flat surface. Noise dominates and telephones ringing like mad seem to bother no one enough to answer them. As soon as one *is* finally answered, another starts ringing. Brokers and clients huddle in the cubicles as though they were in a confessional box without curtains. Sometimes people sit on a pile of telephone books, talking to each other over the deafening clatter. Above your head a lot of figures that look like cryptograms chase each other just underneath the ceiling. These are the stock symbols as they come on the ticker from the stock exchange, giving the latest trading price of each stock indicated. Every listed stock has its own symbol. You might wonder if people can conduct any kind of serious business in a place like this.

Showing an assurance you may not feel, ask the receptionist how to buy a copy of Standard & Poor's *Stock Guide* and *Bond Guide*. They cost about $2.50 each. They are issued monthly, and a guide to reading them comes later on.

Don't let yourself get talked into meeting any of the brokers now. You have some homework to do before you consult a professional, and, besides, you don't want to choose your advisors by random chance. If you don't feel like making such a field trip, you can write for the booklets to Standard & Poor's Corporation, 25 Broadway, New York, NY 10004.

While you're downtown, buy a copy of the *Wall Street Journal* and keep it handy, unless your husband's subscription still brings it to your house. When you have the two booklets on stocks and bonds and the *Wall Street Journal* in hand, you are ready to start an intensive course of self-directed study. Actually you will be doing a research project on the specific investments your husband made that you now hold. Remember the list of stock and bond certificates you made up for the lawyer that is now in your safe-deposit box? Make two copies of it: one for yourself to work with and one for your future investment counselor. Return the original to the box. In general, it is a good policy never to let the original of any paper out of your hands. If you were able to locate your husband's records of his investments, make a copy of these too.

The investment advisor will need them because they should

show the date each stock or bond was purchased, what it cost, what it has paid out since purchase in the form of interest or dividends, and whether any of the stocks split at any time. Stocks are sometimes split two for one, three for two, and sometimes more. When a company decides to split its stock, usually because the price is too high for easy trading, the price of the stock is reduced accordingly; though you will own more shares, their total value is the same as it was before the split was announced. Thus splits are a nice way of acquiring more shares of stock without putting up any additional money.

If you have found the name and phone number of your husband's broker or investment counselor, call for an appointment. If you never did locate his financial guiding light, you may still be thinking over suggestions your lawyer made or recommendations from friends. Call all of them for appointments, but set the dates sometime in the future, after you have completed your copying task. They will want to see the information you have assembled, fully documented.

To keep things simple, let's assume that all your stocks are listed on the New York stock exchange and that they are all common, not preferred, stocks. Preferred stocks are generally less volatile and therefore less interesting for our purposes. *The Wall Street Journal* and Standard & Poor's *Stock Guide* are your texts for the time being. We will set the issue of bonds aside for the moment because bonds are less mysterious. They tell you on their face how much they will be worth when they mature, what the date of maturity will be, what interest they pay, and when they pay it. Stock certificates don't give you that sort of information.

Take a look through the *Stock Guide*. Then look carefully at the two pages from it illustrated here. The stocks are listed alphabetically in the guide, which is issued monthly and lists regularly traded, publicly held stocks on all the exchanges. To

46 Cat-Cen — Standard & Poor's Corporation

Index	Ticker Symbol	Name of Issue (Call Price of Pfd. Stocks)	Market	Com. Rank. & Pfd. Rating	Par Val.	Inst. Hold Cos	Inst. Hold Shs. (000)	Principal Business	1971-83 High	1971-83 Low	1984 High	1984 Low	1985 High	1985 Low	Oct. Sales in 100s	October, 1985 Last Sale Or Bid High	Low	Last	%Div. Yield	P-E Ratio
¶1●[1]	CAT	Caterpillar Tractor	NY,B,C,M,P,Ph	B	No	403	59015	Earthmoving mchy: diesel eng	73¼	25⅝	52⅝	28⅝	38¼	29	41642	37⅝	34⅝	35½	1.4	25
2	CBTB	CB&T Bancshares	OTC	A	2½	8	273	Multi-bank hldg,Georgia	11⅛	2½	16⅝	10⅝	33	13⅝	414	30	26	27B	1.6	21
3	CBH	CBI Indus	NY,M	B+	2½	96	10343	Steel plate structures,tanks	70⅞	7¾	33⅞	24⅛	29	18¼	9617	21⅝	18¼	19¼	3.1	20
¶4●[2]	CBS	CBS Inc	NY,B,C,M,P,Ph	A	2½	319	16949	Broadcasting,records,publish	81¾	24⅝	87¾	61½	125	70⅞	61650	119½	108	118½	2.5	18
5	Pr	$1 cm Cv A Pref (43½)vtg	NY,P	↓A—	1	...	....	Home leisure time prod, toy	53½	17½	58½	44¼	85	52½	5	82	77½	82	1.2	..
6	CCBF	CCB Financial	OTC	A	5	4	1218	Bankhldg:No Carolina	17	3½	24½	16⅝	34¼	24½	287	31	29¾	31B	3.2	10
7	CCBL	C-COR Electrs	OTC	↓B—	10¢	5	40	CATV equip-amplifiers	35¾	9¼	13	6	9½	5½	1203	7½	5½	5½B	...	d
8	CCX	CCX Inc	NY,M,P	↓B—	2	7	411	Wire & cable,alloy steels	11¼	2⅝	10¼	4¼	8½	4	1346	4¾	4	4¼	...	25
9	Pr	5% cm Pfd (27)	NY(10),P	CCC	25	...	....	screening, rubber prdts	17¾	7½	10⅝	8¼	12	9	10	11	10½	10⅝B	11.8	..
10	CDI	CDI Corp	AS	B	10¢	6	655	Engr'g & technical services	11	¼	11⅝	7¾	22⅛	9⅞	459	22⅛	18	21⅝	...	12
11	CDXX	CDX Corp	OTC	NR	1¢	1	18	Computer medic diagnose eq	8⅝	⅝	1	¼	1⅛	¼	411	¼	¼	¼B	...	d
12	CCP	Ceco Indus	NY,M	B	No	28	1593	Construction industry items	26	6⅛	25¾	16	27¾	20	968	25⅞	24¼	25⅞	3.1	10
13	CCL	Celanese Canada	To,Mo,Vc	B—	No	8	858	Fibers,fabrics,chemicals	14½	2½	11⅝	6	10¼	6¼	312	9⅝	8¼	8⅞	2.3	16
¶14●[3]	CZ	Celanese Corp	NY,B,C,M,P,Ph	B+	No	180	6296	Fibers, chemicals, plastics	79¾	24½	62	62⅝	131¼	79¾	10067	131¼	124¾	129¼	3.7	11
15	Pr	4½% cm A Pfd (100)	NY	BBB	100	3	57	paints/indust'l coatings	65¾	30	38¾	34	44¼	37⅝	43	43¾	43	43¼	10.4	..
16	CELP	Cellular Products	OTC	NR	1¢	1	40	Protein substances:R&D,mfr	1 7/16	1	1⅞	1 1/16	4¼	1½	3446	2⅞	1¾	2⅝B	...	d
17	CNCR	CenCor Inc	OTC	B+	1	7	136	Loans:day care:ed:temp help	19¾	½	6¾	4⅝	12½	5⅝	579	12½	10	12¼B	...	14
18	CRG	Cenergy Corp	NY	NR	25¢	41	2978	Oil&gas explor,prod:pipeline	....	....	15	7½	10⅛	7⅝	7676	9⅞	8¾	9⅞	0.4	27
19	CNT	Centel Corp	NY,B,M	A+	2½	242	13681	Telephone,elec,communic sys	40⅝	13	38½	30⅝	45	36½	4824	44¼	40⅞	42⅝	5.6	9
20	CEG	Centennial Group[60]	AS	NR	50¢	1	11	Real estate & development	92½	3⅜	7½	4⅝	9⅜	4⅝	799	9⅝	5¼	9	...	d
21	CTBC	Centerre Bancorp	OTC	A—	10	58	1947	Multiple bank hldg:St Louis	29	10½	29½	18½	35½	26¾	4129	32	29½	31½B	5.7	9
¶22	CTX	Centex Corp	NY,M	B+	25¢	91	9877	R.E.devel,constr,cement,o&g	33⅛	2¾	31½	18	26⅞	20½	5965	23⅞	21½	23⅝	1.1	9
23	CNTO	Centocor Inc	OTC	NR	1¢	34	2101	Develops diagnostic test kits	25½	12¼	16¼	8	20¾	8¼	6543	20¾	16	20B	...	..
24	CFNVF	Centrafarm Group NV	OTC	NR	[illegible]	11	512	Markets pharmaceuticals	....	....	....	....	15⅝	6⅝	5520	13¼	9⅞	12B	...	29
25	CBAN	Cent'l Bancorp'n Cin	OTC	A	5	34	1139	Multiple bank hldg:Cinn	30½	11	37¼	28⅝	57	36¾	879	56¾	53	55B	s3.7	10
26	CBSS	Cent'l Bancshrs South	OTC	A—	2	26	1747	Bank hldg: Alabama	15⅝	3 15/16	12⅝	10 1/16	21½	12¼	7997	21½	17	21B	3.6	10
27	CSYS	Central Banking Sys	OTC	A—	2½	5	54	Bank hldg: California	21⅞	1⅞	21¼	14¾	18¼	15¼	680	16¼	16	16B	s2.5	11
28	CFBS	Central Fidelity Banks	OTC	A+	5	26	2490	Bank holding, Virginia	16⅛	3⅝	19¼	12⅝	31⅛	19	2204	26½	24⅛	24⅞B	3.4	10
29	CNH	Central Hudson Gas&El	NY,M	A	No	38	828	Utility:elec & gas, NY State	27	11	25⅝	16⅛	31¼	23	3494	27	24⅝	26¾	11.1	6
30	Pr	Dep1/4shr Adj Rt[53]A Pfd([55]25.75)	[4]	A—	100	3	131		27	24½	26¼	20¼	27⅝	23½	235	27⅝	27	26B	9.4	..
31	CER Pr	Central Ill Lt 4½% cm Pfd[57]	NY(10)	AA—	100	...	....	Sub of CILCORP:elec/gas util	69	28½	41⅜	36	46	40	16	43	41	41¾	10.8	..
32	CIP	Central Ill Pub Sv	NY,B,C,M,Ph	A—	No	122	8266	Electric & natural gas utility	22⅝	8½	17⅞	14	21½	16¾	7670	19⅞	17⅝	19⅛	8.6	11
33	CJER	Central Jersey Bancorp	OTC	A	2½	3	111	Gen'l comm'l bank'g & trust	21½	6⅞	21¼	17	35¼	20	1085	35¼	30½	34¾B	3.5	12
34	CNL	Central La Elec	NY,M	A—	4	63	2699	Electric sv in Louisiana	19½	12¾	22¼	17⅝	29⅛	21¼	5919	27½	24⅞	26¼	7.9	7
35	Pr	$4.18 cm Pfd([56]31.88)1/4 vtg	NY	BBB+	25	...	....		35	27½	33¾	29⅛	37	32½	177	35½	33⅞	35¼	11.9	..
36	CTP	Central Maine Power[70]	NY,B,M	NR	5	35	925	Utility supplies electricity	21¼	10⅛	14⅜	7⅞	13⅞	9¼	30886	13⅜	12⅞	12¾	11.0	..
37	Pr	3.50% cm Pfd (101)	AS(10)	BB+	100	...	....	oil 50%,nuclear 31%,hyd 19%	53	21⅞	27¼	20⅝	31	23⅝	11	29⅜	27¾	28½	12.3	..
38	CPCO	Central Pacific	OTC	B	No	4	268	Bank hldg: Bakersfield,Cal	19½	6⅞	9¾	4¾	8½	5⅛	1129	7¼	6¼	7¼B	...	32
39	CRLC	Central Reserve Life	OTC	NR	No	...	....	Life,small group health ins	3⅛	⅝	5⅝	2	14	5⅛	1785	11⅞	9	11½B	1.0	11
40	CET	Central Securities	AS	NR	1	6	339	Closed-end investment co	16⅞	2⅞	14⅜	11	14½	11¾	266	12⅝	11¾	12½	1.6	..
41	Pr D	$2.00 cm Cv D Pref(27½)	AS	NR	No	...	....		....	....	25¼	22½	27	23¾	....	....	....	24B	8.3	..
42	CNSP	Central Sprinkler	OTC	NR	1¢	16	576	Mfrs fire sprinkler sys	....	....	....	....	19	12¾	1169	18½	17¾	18½B	...	14
¶43	CSR	Central & So. West	NY,B,C,M,P,Ph	A+	3½	346	41295	Integ elec utility hldg co	26½	10¾	22⅞	16⅞	27	21⅝	34830	25¾	24⅛	25⅝	7.9	7
44	CV	Central Vt Pub Serv	NY,M	A	6	17	730	Electricity in Vt., N.H.	19⅝	5¼	17¼	10⅞	21¾	16½	2568	20½	19⅛	19½	9.7	6
45	CEN	Centronics Data	NY,B,M,Ph	C	1¢	18	944	Mfr computer printers	54⅝	1½	17⅝	7⅝	10⅝	2½	8477	4⅞	4¼	4⅝	...	d
46	CENT	Centuri Inc	OTC	B—	5¢	7	3236	Hunt'g/fish'g eq:seafood prod	13⅜	¼	3⅛	⅞	2	⅞	13490	1⅝	1⅛	1½B	...	d

Uniform Footnote Explanations—See Page 1. Other: [1]AS:Cycle 2. [2]CBOE:Cycle 2. [3]CBOE:Cycle 3. [4]NY. [51]□$0.72,'81. [52]□$0.82,'82. [53]□$0.43,'81. [54]⊛$1.94,'84. [55]□$2.50,'82. [56]⊛$10.07,'84. [57]'40 Wk Mar'83. [58]Stk dstr of LaPetite Academy. [59]Pfd in $M. [60]Investors S&L plans mgr,0.20 Pfd. [61]Stk dstr of Cenergy Corp. [62]Par Dfl 3.33. [63]△$0.14,'82. [64]⊛$1.79,'84. ... [70]Plan form hldg Co,Maine Indus.

Common and Preferred Stocks — Cat-Cen 47

Splits ◆ Index	Cash Divs. Ea. Yr. Since	Dividends: Latest Payment Per$	Date	Ex. Div.	Total $ So Far 1985	Ind. Rate	Paid 1984	Financial Position Mil-$ Cash& Equiv.	Curr. Assets	Curr. Liab.	Balance Sheet Date	Capitalization Lg Trm Debt Mil-$	Shs. 000 Pfd.	Com.	Earnings $ Per Shr. Years End	1981	1982	1983	1984	1985	Last 12 Mos.	Interim Earnings Period	$ Per Shr. 1984	1985	Index
1	1914	Q0.12½	11-20-85	10-15	0.50	0.50	1.25	340.	2964	1665	9-25-85	1348	...	97784	Dc	6.64	d2.04	d3.74	■d4.47	E1.40↑	d1.44	12 Mo Sep	d1.97	d1.44	1
2◆	1930	Q0.11	10-1-85	9-16	0.403	0.44	0.343	Book Value $7.43			6-30-85	16.7	...	11049	Dc	■0.71	■0.66	Δ0.80	■1.10	....	1.26	9 Mo Sep	■0.81	Δ0.97	2
3	1913	Q0.15	12-31-85	11-25	1.20	0.60	†1.55	56.8	336.	247.	7-13-85	288.	...	21560	Dc	4.73	5.06	Δ2.36	2.09	....	0.97	28 Wk Jul	1.35	□0.23	3
4	1931	Q0.75	9-12-85	8-22	2.25	3.00	2.65	96.9	1624	1063	6-30-85	371.	50	p23404	Dc	□[4]6.58	□[4]4.83	6.31	Δ6.59	E6.50↓	5.75	6 Mo Jun	Δ3.73	2.89	4
5	1967	Q0.25	9-30-85	8-22	0.75	1.00	1.00	Conv into 0.6886 shrs common				....	50	...	Dc	b5.34	b4.73	b6.41	b8.96	....	....				5
6◆	1934	Q0.25	1-24-86	12-24	0.89	1.00	0.69½	Book Value $17.24			6-30-85	26.5	...	4192	Dc	■1.26	■1.48	■2.08	2.70	....	3.19	9 Mo Sep	■2.10	■2.59	6
7	.....	None Since Public			....	Nil	....	6.62	21.1	2.72	6-30-85	0.84	...	3005	Je	0.53	1.12	1.05	0.09	0.01	d0.33	3 Mo Sep	0.07	d0.27	7
8◆	.....	0.093	9-1-76	8-6	....	Nil	....	2.91	28.1	8.15	6-30-85	0.60	119	3851	Je	▲1.73	d3.47	d1.49	•0.18	•0.39	0.17	3 Mo Sep	•0.12	•d0.10	8
9	1949	Q0.31¼	12-2-85	11-4	1.25	1.25	1.25	...	...	...		....	119	....	Je	b1.78	b0.97	bd2.64	b2.65	....	....				9
10◆	.....	0.056	11-2-70	10-16	....	Nil	....	0.85	70.7	43.0	7-31-85	26.9	...	3980	Ap	0.58	Δ0.73	0.45	▲1.21	1.53	1.77	3 Mo Jul	0.31	0.55	10
11◆	.....	None Since Public			....	Nil	....	0.04	0.52	0.44	6-30-85	0.01	...	3063	Je	d0.96	d1.08	d0.24	Δd0.18	d0.02	d0.02				11
12◆	1921	Q0.20	1-3-86	12-4	0.76	0.80	0.72	3.69	162.	77.1	6-30-85	16.4	p.	4721	Dc	□[12]3.10	2.11	2.34	[12]2.05	....	2.56	9 Mo Sep	1.46	1.97	12
13	1983	gQ0.05	9-30-85	9-17	g0.15	0.20	g0.20	2.15	154.	65.0	j6-30-85	58.8	495	13537	Dc	Δ1.14	d0.47	0.61	0.40	....	0.55	9 Mo Sep	0.36	0.50	13
14	1939	Q1.20	12-31-85	11-22	4.50	4.80	4.10	167.	1440	992.	6-30-85	609.	914	p12153	Dc	9.01	□[14]0.05	6.89	[14]10.87	E12.00	11.97	9 Mo Sep	8.53	9.63	14
15	1951	Q1.12½	1-1-86	11-22	4.50	4.50	4.50	...	...	...		....	851	...	Dc	b2.93	b0.44	b2.44	b3.01	....	....				15
16	.....	None Since Public			....	Nil	....	0.35	0.78	0.81	6-30-85	0.41	...	4932	Mr	....	[57]d0.03	d0.09	d0.14	....	d0.16	3 Mo Jun	d0.02	d0.04	16
17◆	.....	h[29]....	9-1-83	9-2	....	Nil	....	13.3	105.	34.8	6-30-85	67.0	184	4233	Dc	0.30	0.48	0.82	0.65	....	0.86	9 Mo Sep	0.42	0.63	17
18	1985	Q0.10	10-4-85	8-29	0.04	0.04	....	1.33	23.0	19.3	6-30-85	71.6	300	9739	Mr	0.61	0.69	0.63	0.36	....	0.37	3 Mo Jun	0.07	0.08	18
19	1939	Q0.59½	10-31-85	10-1	2.38	2.38	2.32	70.7	376.	329.	6-30-85	734.	[59]40	27639	Dc	3.89	3.96	4.12	4.42	E4.80	4.59	12 Mo Sep	4.34	4.59	19
20◆	.....	1.25	9-3-74	8-13	....	Nil	....	Equity per shr $5.80			3-31-85	7.26	p.	1359	Je	•0.05	•ΔNil	▲d0.30	Δ•Nil	pΔd0.33	d0.33				20
21	1919	Q0.45	11-30-85	10-30	1.80	1.80	1.80	Book Value $40.13			6-30-85	96.2	...	7697	Dc	■4.61	▲3.05	▲2.74	▲3.05	....	3.42	9 Mo Sep	▲2.27	▲2.64	21
22◆	1973	Q0.06¼	10-7-85	9-3	0.25	0.25	h[61]0.25	Equity per shr $16.86			6-30-85	61.0	...	18459	Mr	1.41	Δ1.84	2.55	2.20	E2.75	2.26	3 Mo Jun	0.61	0.69	22
23	.....	None Since Public			....	Nil	....	12.1	17.3	1.75	3-31-85	....	...	±7197	Dc	±d0.48	±d0.51	±d0.12	•±0.06	....	0.19	9 Mo Sep	±•0.03	±•0.16	23
24	.....	None Since Public			....	Nil	....	6.41	15.6	4.17	3-31-86	1.52	...	*5667	Dc	....	....	....	0.45	....	0.42	6 Mo Jun	0.22	0.19	24
25◆	1937	Q0.51¼	10-7-85	9-23	s2.024	2.05	1.904	Book Value $38.39			6-30-85	24.1	...	5508	Dc	▲■3.35	■3.85	■4.06	▲4.80	....	5.70	9 Mo Sep	▲3.47	▲4.37	25
26◆	1939	Q0.19	10-1-85	9-11	0.73½	0.76	0.64½	Book Value $14.52			6-30-85	6.40	...	13702	Dc	■0.54	▲•[63]1.59	▲1.81	▲[44]1.85	....	2.16	9 Mo Sep	■1.33	▲1.64	26
27◆	1940	Q0.10	10-15-85	9-25	s0.39½	0.40	s0.376	Book Value $17.62			6-30-85	30.4	...	3207	Dc	▲2.06	■1.73	▲2.10	■1.65	....	1.44	9 Mo Sep	1.50	1.29	27
28◆	1969	Q0.21	10-1-85	9-9	0.793	0.84	0.708	Book Value $14.44			6-30-85	47.8	34	13537	Dc	■1.34	■1.58	■2.01	■2.28	....	2.39	9 Mo Sep	■1.70	■1.81	28
29	1903	Q0.74	11-1-85	10-4	2.90	2.96	2.75	2.15	86.4	65.6	6-30-85	*372.	1410	*11912	Dc	3.72	3.91	3.94	4.43	....	4.45	12 Mo Sep	4.50	4.45	29
30	1983	0.59½	10-1-85	9-4	2.89	2.45	2.87¼	...	...	...		....	800	...	Dc	....	....	b2.03	b2.21	....	....	SF 32,000 fr Mr'93,$25			30
31	1936	Q1.12½	1-2-86	12-2	4.50	4.50	4.50	15.4	127.	40.1	6-30-85	309.	±846	13584	Dc	b1.99	b2.19	b2.27	b2.31	....	....				31
32	1947	Q0.41	12-10-85	11-12	1.63	1.64	1.58	96.0	286.	102.	6-30-85	520.	1201	34172	Dc	1.73	1.81	2.33	Δ1.99	....	1.82	12 Mo Sep	Δ1.91	1.82	32
33◆	1925	Q0.30	10-1-85	9-5	1.17½	1.20	1.10	Book Value $18.62			6-30-85	....	...	4225	Dc	Δ2.03	Δ2.72	Δ2.43	[69]2.54	....	2.90	6 Mo Jun	1.11	1.47	33
34	1935	Q0.52	11-15-85	10-29	2.05	2.08	1.90	12.0	46.1	65.3	6-30-85	280.	1294	10928	Dc	2.46	▲2.47	2.85	3.62	....	3.62	12 Mo Jun	3.47	3.62	34
35	1982	Q1.04½	12-1-85	11-8	4.18	4.18	4.18	Red restr (15.20%)to 8-31-87				....	800	...	Dc	....	b1.77	b2.42	b2.54	....	....				35
36	1943	Q0.35	10-31-85	10-4	1.40	1.40	1.82	82.1	175.	124.	6-30-85	484.	1160	22206	Dc	1.81	2.02	2.51	1.99	....	0.12	12 Mo Jun	2.66	■0.12	36
37	1946	Q0.87½	10-1-85	9-4	3.50	3.50	3.50	...	...	...		....	220	....	Dc	b1.66	b1.92	b2.11	b1.81	....	....				37
38◆	1979	0.04	1-30-84	12-23	....	Nil	0.04	Book Value $9.22			12-31-84	p7.60	...	3065	Dc	2.34	▲1.11	0.10	d3.77	....	0.23	9 Mo Sep	▲d3.86	▲0.14	38
39◆	1980	A0.12	4-26-85	4-9	0.12	0.12	0.08	Book Value $3.42			6-30-85	....	...	3584	Dc	•Δ0.17	•0.15	•0.44	0.89	....	1.09	6 Mo Jun	0.23	0.43	39
40	1955	0.17	9-4-85	8-5	[71]1.57	●0.20	[72]1.70	Net Asset Val $13.56			10-25-85	....	222	6885	Dc	§11.50	§14.02	§17.25	§13.57	....	....				40
41	1984	Q0.50	11-1-85	10-7	2.00	2.00	1.25	Cv into 1.916 shrs com				....	223	...	Dc	....	....	....	....	....	....				41
42	.....	None Since Public			....	Nil	....	0.17	15.9	5.87	7-31-85	*20.0	...	1664	Oc	....	....	....	p0.67	E1.30	1.19	9 Mo Jul	p0.36	0.88	42
43	1947	Q0.50½	11-29-85	11-1	2.02	2.02	1.90	n/a	359.	606.	9-30-85	2318	[73]426	94294	Dc	2.54	2.82	3.02	3.43	E3.60↑	3.56	12 Mo Sep	3.52	3.56	43
44◆	1944	Q0.47½	11-15-85	10-25	1.90	1.90	1.82½	16.0	43.1	32.1	6-30-85	131.	442	6376	Dc	2.81	2.85	2.94	3.19	....	3.47	12 Mo Sep	3.30	3.47	44
45	.....	0.05	1-27-81	12-22	....	Nil	....	43.5	137.	67.3	6-30-85	48.8	...	11752	Dc	■d4.06	[74]d2.94	d0.68	•d0.95	....	d0.56	9 Mo Sep	•d0.44	•d0.05	45
46	.....	None Paid			....	Nil	....	1.28	60.8	46.4	6-30-85	7.53	8	16281	Dc	•0.46	[75]d0.29	•0.15	□d0.06	....	d0.20	6 Mo Jun	•□0.15	•0.01	46

◆ Stock Splits & Divs By Line Reference Index. [2]2-for-1,'84:3-for-2,'85. [6]2-for-1,'84. [8]10%,'81. [10]2-for-1,'84:3-for-2,'85. [11]1-for-6 REVERSE,'85. [12]3-for-2,'84. [17]3-for-1,'85. [20]1-for-5 REVERSE,'85. [22]3-for-2,'83:No adj for Canergy Corp spinoff. [25]Adj to 5%,'85(ex'84). [26]2-for-1,'85. [27]Adj to 5%,'85(ex'84). [28]3-for-2,'83,'85. [33]Adj to 4%,'81. [38]3-for-2,'82. [39]3-for-2,'85. [44]4-for-3,'83.

see how the *Guide* works, let's take a look at the stock of Caterpillar Tractor. It has an interesting recent history. You can see by the number of shares your husband bought that he thought highly of this company. Let's say he had a thousand shares.

We will omit some of the detailed information given on these two sheets and stick to the most important items. Starting on the left side of the left-hand page, underline Caterpillar Tractor all the way across both pages to make it easy to follow. First, you see the symbol CAT. This is used on the stock exchange ticket, that electronic marvel that spews out the latest price changes of each stock as its shares are traded during the business day of the stock exchange, which is 10 a.m. to 4 p.m. eastern time. What you saw happening in the brokerage office was the stock symbols moving along the top of the wall. That symbol is not the same as the abbreviation used in the stock market pages of your daily paper or the *Wall Street Journal*. For example, the stock we are following, Caterpillar Tractor, is CatrpT in the stock market page listing.

In 1981 the *Guide* would have told you that the company was rated A, which means high. By 1984 it was dropped to B +. It makes earth moving machinery and diesel engines. Next, it gives you the high and low prices at which the stock was traded, that is bought and sold, over a ten-year period. A high of 73 and a low of 25. Maybe your husband was lucky enough to have bought it somewhere near 25.

Next come the highs and lows for the last two years; then the percent the divident represents to the price of the stock. If, for example, a stock is selling at 10 and it is paying $1, the yield is 10%. If it is selling at 10 and paying $.50, the yield is 5%. The prices quoted are in dollars, though the word is seldom used. So when a stock is said to be selling at

10, it is selling at $10 per share. All of that is simple enough. It's just the kind of arithmetic you learned in school.

On the right-hand page you learn that Caterpillar has been sending out dividend checks each year since 1914. This indicates the company is pretty well entrenched in the economy. On the left-hand side of the right-hand page, it gives you the amount and date of the last dividend paid. Further along to the right you learn the earnings history for the previous four years. It was very good indeed in 1981. Earnings were $6.64 a year and the dividend was $2.40. Then it went into a deficit (loss) spin. Badly hurt by our government's prohibition to participate in the construction of the Soviet pipeline, the recession, the expensive U.S. dollar compared to the Japanese yen, plus a long strike, Caterpillar cut its dividend in half. In 1984 it was halved again, and as mentioned above, by publication date Caterpillar's rating had been dropped to B+ and the stock fell to 31.

In brief, this is a profile of what politics, foreign exchange, and domestic economic slowdown and no doubt internal management problems, can do to a hitherto strong and stable corporation with an excellent reputation.

What a company earns per share is closely related to what it pays out per share, but it is not one and the same. If the earnings don't go up, you can be pretty sure the dividends won't go up either—and more or less vice versa, although a company will do a lot of other cutting before it cuts its dividend, much less eliminate it altogether. It has to be pretty much of a basket case before the latter happens.

To understand the tie-in between earnings per share and dividends per share, let's look at a hypothetical example. If a company spends $1 to make and sell a pen, but actually sells the pen for $2, the company makes a profit of $1 on each pen sold. At the next quarterly meeting, the board of directors of the company discusses the profits. The scenario might go something like this: the president of the company gets a raise, the director's fees are upped, and then they decide to build a new unit or beef up the research and development department. They might even consider using some of the money to buy another company.

After all the decisions about expenditures have been made, a profit of $.25 per share remains. The board decides to pass this along to the owners of the company, the shareholders. You are now one of these many owners, and the money paid out is a dividend. Once a publicly owned company starts paying dividends, they are very reluctant to stop. If there are any dividends, they are declared quarterly at the meeting of the company's board, and they are reported immediately in the *Wall Street Journal* under "Dividend News."

Since dividends are paid quarterly, that is, every three months, simply multiply the amount of the last declared dividend by four to get the amount you might reasonably *expect* to be paid per share in the coming year. In our Caterpillar case, you then multiply by 1,000 whatever the annual dividend was because that is the number of shares you own for purposes of this discussion. This will give you the total amount of return from the stock for the *last* year. The quarterly dividend at the time of this writing was $.125 per share, or $.50 per year. For you, this means $500 a year, since you have 1,000 shares. That means $125 in February, May, August, and November on the 20th of the month as indicated in *Stock Guide*. But of course, who knows about next year?

Those figures in the *Stock Guide* at first may look strange to you. Don't be in a hurry; the more you look at them the more the figures will convey. After all, you are learning a foreign language. Take in what you can; the information will keep and will be there when you need it.

After you complete this exercise—perhaps with a break for some less complex activities—look up all the other common stocks whose certificates you found in the safe-deposit box. Do the same search and study for each of them, and you will get an estimated total of the income to be derived from your stock investments at the present time. These stocks represent a part of the investment portfolio you have to manage, and live on for the rest of your life.

You have assessed the recent past performance of these investments. Next you want to know how much the stocks are worth, what they are selling for today. In the *Wall Street Journal,* in the back, the stocks are listed under the heading, "NYSE Composite Transactions." At the top of each column are a series of brief headings—"52 week High and Low" which gives you the stock's selling range for the previous 12 months. Sometimes the spread is big, sometimes quite narrow. Next comes the previous quarterly dividend quoted at the annual rate, which you already know about, then the percent of yield. If the price of the stock went up after the last dividend was declared, the yield will go down, since the dividend was fixed for a quarter at least. Similarly, if the price went down and the dividend remains the same, the yield percentage will go up. This is explained in more detail later on.

The next column gives the P/E. The significance of the P/E is explained later. Next comes the number of shares bought and sold that day, called "transactions." For every buyer, there is a seller and vice versa. Then under "High, Low and Close" the extremes of the price changes during that business day and the price at which that particular stock ended the day are given. Under "net change," you see how much the stock went up or down from the opening price that day.

To find the worth of each stock, simply multiply the closing price by the number of shares the certificates say you have of any given company; this represents the value of the holding. Caterpillar Tractor, for instance at this writing, closed at 31½ or $31.50. Since theoretically you have a thousand shares, your stock in the company was then worth a thousand times $31.50 or $31,500.

Once you have the names and identifications of your stocks, the dividends expected and the worth of each, you are ready to start tracking their current performance. This process will tell you how each stock does over a period of time, and it will help you make intelligent investment decisions in the future. The proper tools for tracking your securities are simple: a calculator, a looseleaf binder with 8½x11 lined paper, a pen, a ruler, and maybe a magnifying glass if your local paper insists on running the whole New York Stock Exchange Report on one page. The *Wall Street Journal* uses more space than that and is therefore easier to read.

A straightforward method of keeping this sort of record is to enter the company's market page abbreviation and the number of shares you have of its stock on the left-hand side of the page. Skip a line between entries as you go down the page. You might decide later on to enter some other information, such as the dividends paid. Next, ruler in hand, ink in vertical lines no more than half an inch apart, as many as the page will hold. Enter the latest price quoted for each stock in the first column after its name and put the date at the top of each column. If you list the stocks alphabetically, it will be much simpler, but you can also do it any other way that suggests itself to you. The objective is to make the price changes easy for you to follow.

The growing minicomptuer business offers electronic toys for this purpose that are even tax deductible. For example, there are many specific software programs for the Apple II. If you get seriously into this subject, you might find a computer both worthwhile and fun.

New York Stock Exchange Issues

CONSOLIDATED TRADING

TUESDAY, NOVEMBER 19, 1985

52-Week High	52-Week Low	Stock	Div	Yld %	PE Ratio	Sales 100s	High	Low	Last	Chg.
24⅞	19½	BorgWa	.96	4.2	12	2442	23¼	22⅝	23⅛	+ ⅜
10⅝	4⅝	Bormns		...	14	79	10	9⅞	10	+ ⅜
44⅛	33	BosEd	3.44	8.2	8	349	42	41⅜	41¾	+ ⅜
85	67⅜	BosE pf	8.88	10.8	...	z120	82¼	82	82	− ½
11½	9¾	BosE pr	1.17	10.6	...	30	11⅛	11	11	− ⅛
14⅛	11½	BosE pr	1.46	10.4	...	67	14	13⅞	14	+ ⅛
25⅞	19¾	Bowatr	.72	3.1	9	785	23	22⅞	22⅞	...
31⅛	25¾	BrigSt	1.60	5.9	13	272	27⅜	27⅛	27⅛	...
66½	47¼	BristM	1.88	3.0	17	1829	62⅞	61⅞	62¼	− ¼
4⅞	3⅝	BritLnd		...	...	15	3¾	3¾	3¾	− ⅛
33½	21⅜	BritPt	2.01e	5.9	9	873u	34⅛	33⅝	34	+ ¾
28¾	22	BrtT2 pp	.61e	2.2	13	26	27⅝	27½	27⅝	+ ¼
4	1	Brock		...	...	198	1⅛	1	1	− ⅛
29⅞	16⅞	Brckwy	1.32	4.6	14	273	29	28½	28⅞	+ ⅜
43⅜	34⅞	BkyUG	3.12	7.5	8	33	41¾	41⅜	41½	...
37¼	30⅝	BkUG pf	3.95	11.4	...	31	34¾	34⅛	34½	+ ¼
26¾	16	BwnSh	.20	.9	15	11	22⅜	22¼	22⅜	+ ⅛
36¾	25	BrwnGp	1.36	4.0	22	223	34⅝	33⅞	33⅞	− ⅛
59¼	32¾	BrwnF	1.08	1.9	19	524	59⅛	58¼	58⅜	− ⅜
40¾	28¼	Brnswk	1.00	2.5	9	416	40¼	39⅞	40⅛	+ ⅜
40⅜	29¼	BrshWl	.52	1.7	14	141	31⅞	31⅛	31½	− ¼
19½	16	Bundy	.80	4.3	66	15	18½	18⅛	18½	+ ⅜
20	16½	BunkrH	2.16	11.3	..	6	19⅛	19⅛	19⅛	...
20¼	14¼	BurlnCt		...	12	122	16	15⅝	16	+ ¼
32	24¼	Burlind	1.64	5.2	72	262	31⅞	31½	31⅝	...
68⅞	45	BrlNth	1.40	2.1	9	619	67⅝	66⅞	67	− ⅝
7⅞	6⅜	BrlNo pf	.55	7.5	...	7	7⅜	7⅜	7⅜	...
24⅛	19⅞	BrlN pf	2.12	8.9	...	1	23¾	23¾	23¾	− ¼
52	47¾	BrlN pf	5.10e	10.2	...	47	50	49⅝	49⅝	...
18¼	9⅜	Burndy	.44	4.0	39	185	11	10⅞	10⅞	− ⅛
68	52	Burrgh	2.60	4.4	12	1551	59⅛	58⅜	59⅛	+ ⅜
20⅜	11	Butlrln	.52	3.6	17	533	14½	14¼	14½	+ ⅜
5¼	1	Buttes		...	...	902	1¼d	¾	¾	− ⅜
12⅞	2	Butes pf	1.05k	...	...	67	1⅞d	1¾	1¾	− ¼
29	18¼	CBI In	.60	3.2	...	341	19	18¾	19	− ⅛
126¼	68⅞	CBS	3.00	2.6	...	2069	119¼	116½	116½	−2¼
8½	4	CCX		...	10	47	5	4⅞	5	...
12	9	CCX pf	1.25	11.9	...	z100	10½	10½	10½	− ¼
63⅛	38	CIGNA	2.60	4.3	26	1028	61⅝	60⅝	60¾	− ¾
33¼	26¼	CIG pf	2.75	8.5	...	86	32⅝	32⅛	32¼	− ¼
54¾	49	CIG pf	4.10	7.5	...	101	54⅝	54¼	54⅝	+ ⅛
6½	1⅜	CLC		...	...	45	1⅞	1⅞	1⅞	...
63¼	28½	CNA Fn		...	12	228	63	61½	62	−1⅛
11¾	9⅞	CNAI	1.24	10.7	...	42	11¾	11½	11⅝	+ ¼
28⅞	16¼	CNW		...	...	873	17⅞	17	17⅜	− ⅜
52¼	38¼	CPC Int	2.20	4.3	17	675	51⅜	50½	51	− ⅛
27⅝	17⅜	CP Ntl	1.50	5.6	10	89	27	26⅜	26⅞	+ ¼
22⅜	19½	CRIIMI	2.26e	11.1	...	198	20⅝	20¼	20⅜	+ ⅛
19⅜	14¼	CRS	.34	2.2	14	48	16	15¾	15¾	− ⅛
28⅞	21⅜	CSX	1.16	4.1	10	10014	28¾	28⅛	28¼	...
40¼	27½	CTS	1.00	3.2	11	34	31¼	30⅞	31¼	+ ⅜
12½	7⅜	C 3 Inc		...	225	128	9	8¾	9	+ ⅛
33¾	20½	Cabot	.92	3.6	...	347	26⅛	25⅞	25⅞	− ⅛
17⅜	8⅞	Caesar		...	14	626	15⅛	14⅞	15⅛	+ ⅛
25⅞	13¾	CalFed	.48	2.0	4	1126	24¼	23⅝	23¾	− ¼
54¼	38½	CalFd pf	4.75	8.8	...	449	54¼	53¼	54	+ ½
21	13½	Callhn	.25b	1.3	...	98	20	19⅛	20	+ ⅞
32⅝	19¼	Calmat	.60	1.9	15	57	32½	32⅛	32⅛	− ½
15⅞	12	Camrnl	.12	.9	41	39	13¼	13	13⅛	...
26	15¼	CRLk g	.40	...	...	227	23⅜	22⅞	23⅛	− ⅛
5⅜	2⅛	CmpR g	.16i	...	...	295	2⅝	2½	2⅝	...
46½	30⅛	CamSp s	1.25	2.8	14	294	45⅝	45	45⅝	+ ⅛
15⅞	11⅝	CdPac s	.48	...	...	379	12⅝	12½	12⅝	+ ¼
22¼	17½	CanPE g	.80	...	11	24	20⅝	20½	20⅝	+ ⅛
228½	151	CapCits	.20	...	20	160	215	211¼	213	−1
27⅝	19⅞	CapHd s	.77	3.0	9	184	25½	25⅛	25⅜	+ ⅛
12⅜	9	Caring g	.48	...	...	99	9⅝	9⅝	9⅝	+ ¼
40¼	27¼	Carlisle	1.08	3.5	10	404	31⅛	30¼	31	+ ⅜
27⅞	18⅛	CaroFt	.40	1.5	12	444	27⅛	26⅜	26¾	+ ⅛
30⅜	24	CarPw	2.60	9.1	7	953	28⅞	27¾	28½	− ⅛
26¾	21⅜	CarP pf	2.67	10.6	...	11	25⅝	25¼	25¼	− ⅛
48	29⅜	CarTec	2.10	6.6	15	146	31⅞	31¼	31⅞	+ ⅞
11½	6½	Carrol	.10	1.4	11	82	7⅛	7	7⅛	+ ⅛
26½	17¾	CarPir s	.60	2.4	10	x344	25¼	24¼	25¼	+1¼
31	22½	CartHw	1.22	4.3	18	109	28¾	28½	28⅝	...
46⅞	24¾	CartWl	.60	1.3	13	129	46¼	45⅞	46¼	...
18½	12⅞	CascNG	1.20	7.4	8	69	16¼	16	16⅛	− ⅛
16⅜	9⅛	CastlCk		...	...	696	12⅝	12⅜	12⅝	+ ¼
28⅜	15¾	CstlC pf	1.88k	...	...	12	27¼	27	27	+ ⅛
15⅝	12	CstlC pf	.90	6.1	...	305	14⅞	14⅝	14¾	− ⅛
39⅛	28⅜	CalrpT	.50	1.3	...	7111u	39⅝	38½	39	+ ¾
29	19⅜	Ceco	.80	2.9	11	50	28	27⅝	27¾	− ¼
133¾	74⅞	Celanse	4.80	3.6	11	422	133½	132½	133½	+1¼
44⅜	36	Celan pf	4.50	10.0	...	14u	45⅛	44½	45⅛	+ ⅞
10½	7⅜	Cengy	.04e	.5	22	86	8⅜	8¼	8¼	− ¼
45½	34¾	Centel	2.38	5.3	10	120	45⅛	44½	44¾	− ⅜
26⅞	20½	Centex	.25	1.0	11	197	24⅜	24¼	24⅜	+ ⅜
27	20⅞	CenSoW	2.02	7.8	7	1206	25⅞	25¾	25⅞	...
31¼	23	CenHud	2.96	10.7	6	101	28	27¾	27¾	− ⅛
21½	16⅛	CntlPS	1.64	8.4	11	228	19⅝	19¼	19½	+ ⅛
29⅛	20½	CnLaEl	2.08	7.8	7	91	27⅛	26¾	26¾	− ⅛
37	31¾	CLaEl pf	4.18	11.9	...	1	35	35	35	+ ¼
13⅞	9⅛	CeMPw	1.40	10.9	107	277	13	12⅞	12⅞	− ⅛
21¾	16⅜	CVIPS	1.90	9.4	6	82	20¼	20	20¼	+ ¼
11⅛	2½	CentrDt		...	...	532	4½	4⅜	4½	...
12⅜	8¾	CntryTl	.80	6.3	9	163u	12⅞	12½	12¾	+ ⅛
23	17⅛	Cenvill	2.40	14.9	7	279	17¾d	16⅛	16⅛	−1⅜
28½	19¾	Crt-teed	.70	2.8	9	605	25	24½	24⅝	− ⅛
30½	16½	CessAir	.30i	...	28	7	30⅛	29⅞	30⅛	+ ¼
25⅜	19	Chmpln	.52	2.3	...	3871	23¼	22¾	23	+ ⅛
27⅝	22	Chml pf	1.20	5.0	...	4	24½	24	24	− ¼
54½	46⅜	Chml pf	4.60	8.7	...	60	52¾	52¼	52⅝	+ ¼
9⅞	7¾	ChamSp	.40	4.6	15	x319	8⅞	8⅝	8¾	+ ⅛
4⅛	1	viChrtC		...	...	147	2⅜	2¼	2⅜	+ ⅛
4⅛	1½	viChrt pf		...	...	35	2⅞	2¾	2⅞	...
63⅞	41⅞	Chase	3.80	6.2	5	2309	61½	60⅝	61⅜	+ ¾
50	40½	Chase pf	5.25	10.7	...	5	49⅝	49¼	49¼	− ½
56⅜	51½	Chase pf	6.55e	11.8	...	131	55⅝	55¼	55½	+ ⅛
56⅜	51½	Chase pf	8.83e	16.7	...	208	52⅞	52½	52⅞	+ ½
24	16⅞	Chelsea	.72	3.0	10	49	23⅞	23⅜	23¾	− ⅛
32¼	24⅝	Chemed	1.52	5.0	13	42	30¼	30⅛	30¼	+ ¼
44½	31	ChmNY	2.48	6.1	5	1380	40⅝	40¼	40½	+ ⅜
44¼	38¾	ChNY pf	1.87	4.7	...	2	40⅛	40⅛	40⅛	+ ⅜
39½	32	Chespk	1.24	3.4	13	69	36¾	36½	36⅝	...
44¼	31	ChesPn	2.00	4.7	13	2984	42⅜	41⅜	42⅛	...
40¾	29¼	Chevrn	2.40	6.3	9	2082	38½	37⅝	38⅛	− ¼
209	124	ChiMlw		...	71	21	141¼	140¾	141	+ ¾
29⅜	16⅝	ChiPnT	.40e	1.7	12	310	23¼	22⅞	22⅞	− ⅜
11¾	7¼	ChkFull	.24t	3.0	263	102	8	7⅞	7⅞	...
58¾	31	ChrisCr		...	599	90	53⅞	53⅜	53⅞	+ [illegible]
13⅛	7⅜	Christn		...	...	23	10½	10⅜	10⅜	− ¼
17⅜	9⅜	Chroma		...	...	664	17	15¾	15¾	−1¼
79	44¼	Chrm pf	10.00k	...	...	94	76½	75½	75½	−1
45¼	25⅜	Chryslr	1.00	2.3	3	3518	45	43¾	44⅛	−1
54⅛	30½	Chubb s		...	13	747	53	52	52⅜	− ⅜
67½	50¾	Chubb pf	4.25	6.4	...	85	66⅝	66⅜	66⅝	+ ⅛
20¼	13¾	Church s	.44	2.5	15	2573	17⅞	17⅜	17⅞	+ ⅛
11¼	5½	Chyron	.10	1.3	24	93	7¾	7½	7½	− ¼
27¼	21	Citcorp	2.22	8.8	10	293	25¼	25	25¼	+ ⅛
51	40	CinBell	3.12a	6.1	9	13	50¾	50½	50¾	+ ¼
19½	13½	CinGE	2.16	11.1	7	1257	19½	19	19½	+ ⅜
34⅛	27½	CinG pf	4.00	11.9	...	z50	33¾	33¾	33¾	− ¼
75½	61¾	CinG pf	9.28	12.4	...	z1680	75½	75	75	− ½
77	60½	CinG pf	9.52	12.4	...	z200	76½	76½	76½	...
26⅜	15⅛	CinMil	.72	3.9	...	713	18¾	18¼	18⅜	+ ⅛
24⅜	19⅛	CircK s	.50	2.5	...	1320	19¾	19⅜	19¾	+ ⅛
31	18⅜	CirCity	.10	.5	12	283	22¾	22	22	− ⅜
30⅜	15	Circus		...	13	77	25⅜	25	25⅜	...
51¾	34¼	Citicrp	2.26	5.0	6	8075	45¾	45⅛	45½	+ ⅜
84½	70	Citicp pf	7.25e	9.3	...	698	78¼	78	78	+ ¼
8¾	6⅛	Clabir	.72	8.3	6	811u	8⅝	8¼	8⅝	+ ⅜
19¾	6⅜	ClairS s	.10	1.1	18	2120	9⅝	8⅞	9⅛	+ ⅜
32¾	23⅜	ClarkE	1.10	4.5	...	432	25	24½	24⅝	...
14	8½	ClayH s		...	11	51	13¼	13	13⅛	+ ⅛
22¼	16⅜	ClvClf	1.00	5.5	11	44	18¼	17¾	18¼	+ ⅜
21¾	19¾	ClvCl pf	2.00	10.0	...	x18	20	19¾	20	+ ⅜
23⅞	18¼	ClevEl	2.64	11.2	7	2505	23⅝	23¼	23½	− ⅛
64	53	ClvEl pf	7.40	12.1	...	z80	62½	61¼	61¼	+ ⅜
64¼	54½	ClvEl pf	7.56	12.0	...	z200	63	63	63	+1
14½	7¾	Clevpk	.38i	...	...	134	7⅞d	7⅜	7¾	− ⅛
17¾	10	Clvpk pf	1.11j	...	...	10	10¾	10½	10½	− ⅜
18¼	9	Clvpk pf	.92j	...	...	472	9⅛d	8¼	8½	− ⅝
46¼	27½	Clorox	1.36	3.0	13	521	46⅛	45¾	45⅞	− ¼
26⅜	14⅜	ClubMd	.20a	1.0	...	98	20¾	20¼	20¾	+ ½
39⅛	25½	CluettP	1.00	2.6	20	830	39¼	39⅛	39⅛	− ⅛
24¾	16¼	Cluet pf	1.00	4.1	...	5	24⅝	24⅝	24⅝	...
21¼	9⅞	Coachm	.40	3.4	14	224	11⅞	11⅜	11⅜	+ ¼
36¾	16½	Coastl s	.40	1.1	12	3075	36	34⅛	35⅜	+1¼
80½	59½	CocaCl	2.96	3.7	16	2116	80⅛	79⅜	79¾	...
21½	10⅛	Coleco		...	...	1480	19¼	19	19⅛	− ⅛
32⅜	25¼	Colemn	1.20	4.2	19	40	28¾	28½	28⅝	− ⅛

It isn't wise to chart your stocks every day unless you are passionately curious or very nervous about them. Above all, don't let the performance of a stock over a short period of time—less than a couple of months—send you into a state of euphoria or depression. All you are doing at this stage is taking the stock's temperature, so to speak, watching its general health to get some basic understanding of what J.P. Morgan meant when he said the stock market fluctuates.

With your stock record-keeping system set up, you are ready to start looking for the essential background information you need. You will want to read the *Wall Street Journal* with some frequency. In addition to its valuable financial news, it is an excellent general newspaper unless you have a "thing" for crime news. The *Journal* doesn't print crime news except colossal stories like the shooting of the Pope or President.

Using the *Journal* as your textbook, you will discover all sorts of information. Seek out the "Earnings Report" and "Dividend News" sections in the front page index; you can glean very condensed quarterly reports here before they arrive in the mail. The "Annual Meetings Briefs" are worth a glance in case something newsworthy has happened to one of your companies. On the next to last page, second section, are two informative departments called "Abreast of the News" and "Heard on the Street." The first discusses the market's performance the day before and some of the reasons for it, quoting established practitioners in the special fields. You will notice if you read this section regularly, that the experts often disagree as experts do in any other field. A quick consensus is, in fact, rare. The "Heard in the Street" section usually covers the most recent performances of a few selected stocks in some depth.

Reading the *Journal* may make you feel that you need to

PRICE CHANGES
1985
Stocks & Debentures

STOCKS	# SHARES	Cost	1/15	2/9	5/13	6/4	11/19	New Price $
American Home	600	28	53¼	56	61¾	65⅜	59⅜	35,640
Amoco	500	40	53½	59¾	64⅜	62¼	65⅞	32,900
A.T. Cross (ASE)	1000	30½	27¾	30⅜	31	—	33¼	33,250
Ft. Howard Paper	1000*S*	49½	64½	63⅝	68¾	74⅝	46⅜*S*	46,375
Heinz *S*	1800	26	44½	43⅞	47	53¼	32⅜*S*	58,275
IBM	328	54½	124¾	137¼	130⅛	129⅛	138½	45,428
Merck	300	42⅝	94¾	95⅞	102	107¾	121⅝	36,480
M.M.M	400	50⅜	81¼	85½	77	75⅛	80	32,000
Pitney Bowes	1000	30¼	36⅜	40½	39¾	42½	44⅞	44,875
Rubbermaid *S*	800	21	46½	48¾	48½	48⅞	31⅞*S*	25,500
Wisc. E.&P.	1350	32⅜	32⅜	31⅝	35½	—	37⅜	50,490
								411,213

DEBENTURES	Cost	5/13	11/19	New Price $
25 K Mart 6s '99	84	106½	103½	25,875
30 Lomas & Nett. 9s '10	117	109	114	34,200
				60,075
			Total	471,288

S = Stock Split, each 2 for 1

expand your vocabulary. What is "The Dow"; who are the "institutional buyers and sellers"; what are "interest-sensitive" stocks, consumer sectors, asset-play and energy-related issues? What is the money supply, M1 and M2, the "Fed"? Unfortunately, no one source gives a lucid definition of all these and the dozens of other esoteric terms that are commonly used in talking about investments, money, and the economy. Steady reading of the *Journal* and the financial pages of your local daily will eventually translate many of these terms simply by their contexts. A dictionary may be some help too, but Sylvia Porter's column, "Your Money," is likely to be more helpful because she mentions a lot of financial, technical terms but does not use them exclusively. *The Dictionary of Business and Finance* is hard to find, but it's a very useful source, published by Thomas Y. Crowell. Another good resource is Sloan and Zurcher's *Dictionary of Economics*, published by Barnes and Noble. Although the business and finance sections of the weekly news magazines and the financial section of your daily paper are generally easier to understand than the *Wall Street Journal*, they carry far less information of the sort you need. They are good as appetizers, but no substitute for a whole meal. Sylvia Porter's *Money Book* is a very useful reference tool. However, in hardback it weighs five pounds on the bathroom scale—hardly something for light reading in bed. You may feel like exploring other sources of information as well. The financial pages occasionally have advertisements about courses for women dealing with money and investing. Some will be good, and some will only expand your vocabulary. Courses like these or one-day seminars are offered at local community colleges too. Your area may have a women's center that sponsors financial courses just for women. If you can locate a woman in the investment business, she can probably steer you to these courses because she probably lectures at them occasionally.

One bonus from taking some of these courses is that you find you are not unique. In fact, a lot of women know a lot less than you do. The widow of the president of a very large bank attended one such course. She undoubtedly had access to all the financial advice the bank's gallery of talent could offer, but she wanted to find things out for herself. It wasn't that she didn't trust them, but she decided personal comprehension was the only way she could gain peace of mind about the management of her money.

"I didn't feel I could afford, psychologically, to be ignorant any longer about investments," she said. "Handling money isn't like driving a car. I don't understand how cars work either, but I know that if it starts and I keep gas in it and take it to be serviced from time to time, it will probably get me around all right. Money is a lot more complicated because it is subject to forces I not only can't control but know very little about. These days I worry about such cosmic matters as what would happen to the market if there was a revolution in Saudi Arabia. I guess domestic oil stocks would soar, and the multinationals would fall out of bed to the extent that they are involved in Saudi oil production."

Though she talked about a brand new set of things to worry about, she appeared to be thoroughly enjoying herself. She said she felt more confident and in tune with the flow of events around the world as she paid more attention to them now. Perhaps she held a lot of shares in gas and oil—energy stocks.

Another way to build your vocabulary is by watching the weekly TV series *Wall Street Week* on public television. If you view it regularly, you will begin to recognize that they are speaking a specialized form of English, and it will soon

start making sense. This is not said in jest. For a woman t
whom money was only something to spend rather tha
conserve and build on, wading into the jargon of the financia
world is at least as difficult as a self-taught course in French
It is, however, infinitely more rewarding because you can us
this new language every day without having to leave th
country.

The indispensable tool that makes your study and researcl
of money a lot more fun is, of course, the calculator. With it
you can readily measure the ebb and flow of your finances i
the most concrete terms—dollars. As previously mentioned
the numbers given after the name of a stock, under high, low
and close, are of course dollars. Points are also dollars, as i
"IBM went up 2½ points today."

Questions will inevitably come up. Try to keep a list of an
questions and terms, such as equity, leverage, and capita
gains, that you may not understand as you read and stud
You can save them up for your first session with the broker c
financial counselor you choose. Or you may find as you g
along that you are able to cross some things off your lis
because you've gained an understanding of them as you rea
further.

As you pursue your reading and follow the financial page
with increased attention, you will notice that some relatio
ship exists between interest rates, gold prices, internation
events, the issuance of various government reports, domesti
political and economic trends, and your target area of study–
the stock market. For instance, the price of gold tends to g
up with increasing international tensions, and the price c
stocks tends to fall. The recent policy of the independe
governmental body called the Federal Reserve Board (th
Fed) has been aimed at reducing the rate of inflation in th
country. It does this by tightening the supply of money, whic
makes it more expensive to borrow and therefore seriousl

and negatively impacts certain industries, such as housing and the purchase of automobiles. This, in turn, creates pockets of unemployment in parts of the country where the related lumber industry has been the basis of the local economy, or where steel or cars are made. On the other hand, while inflation may be brought under control, excessive interest rates due to a tight money policy also affect government policies and the size of the federal and other budgets and budget deficits. When the cost of U.S. Treasury borrowing is high due to high interest rates, the portion of the federal debt simply to pay the *interest* on the federal debt increases the cost of running the government. And the interest on the federal debt is paid by you and me from our taxes. Louis Rukeyser describes the role of the Federal Reserve Board in *How to Make Money in Wall Street* as an independent agency that likes to operate in conditions of secrecy approximating those of the CIA. "Investors pay close attention not only to interest rates but to any changes in the behavior of the Federal Reserve Board, the independent government agency that may or may not be working in tandem with the administraton of the day. Hints as to its possible shifts of policy regarding the money supply and interest rates often draw conflicting interpretations."

The "Fed" policies affect the amount of reserves a bank must keep in relation to their deposits; hence higher reserves mean "tighter," more expensive money. Perhaps this explains the concern of those who oppose lowered tax rates because that requires the federal Treasury to borrow more and more to take up the differences between its revenue and expenses, thus increasing the national debt to levels formerly unimaginable. This then rocks the financial markets and makes borrowing by industry more expensive because it has to compete with the government for a limited amount of available money, and the U.S. Government is in a highly favorable position to borrow money from all over the world.

A simpler example of the interconnectedness of events is what happens whenever the OPEC countries get together to discuss the selling price and level of production of their oil. This affects the countries that use it to fuel their cars and their utility plants, to cool or heat their houses, and to fertilize their crops. There is a global sigh of relief if the price goes down; energy stocks in general slide and a gallon of gas may drop half a cent.

As your awareness of the interlock of these forces becomes clearer, it will increase your interest in many new areas. Like the banker's widow, you will be inclined to pay more attention to national and international news because it has an impact on your money. It can be fun to follow the day's news and make bets with yourself about how the sum total of events will move the market—up, down, or not at all. Occasionally you will be right and feel pretty good about your growing grasp on the state of matters financial.

When you have done enough studying on your own and have begun to feel comfortable with the language of Wall Street, you will no longer feel overwhelmed by the vernacular of the trade nor awed by the expertise of financial advisers. You might feel ready to consult someone, but first you need to know about some of the various professionals available. They can help you solve your investment problems, develop realistic goals and—with good management and an upbeat investment climate—improve your financial condition. I have described these professionals in random order. You have to decide which services best meet your needs and means.

The *financial planner* is usually called a "certified" financial planner, and this designation implies both course work and an examination for certification. Financial planners get at the whole business of estate planning as well as the acquisition and management of assets (everything you have including your home) as you go along. They deal with your estate, insurance, investments such as stocks and bonds, real estate and the value of any pension or profit-sharing plan. Financial planners have begun to play an increasing role in money management, especially to serve individuals with large assets and high incomes. Some corporations now offer such management and consulting services to their highly paid executives so that their executives can concentrate on the company's business instead of their own and still feel secure about their personal interests.

An *estate planner* analyzes your financial situation with the goal of maximizing the benefits to your heirs so they will pay the least possible tax on their inheritance. An estate planner gets heavily into the taxes on dying governed by both federal and state laws. Consequently this is largely the bailiwick of lawyers, though insurance agents can get into estate planning as well.

Investment counselors charge a certain percent of the assets they manage as their fee. Generally speaking they are individuals in firms that range in size from one person to as many as several hundred with branch offices in various cities. They deal with clients and manage the portfolio or investment holdings a person has. They advise individuals, trusts, pension and profit-sharing plans on stock and bond investments. Some investment counselors also get into real estate, precious metals, and other types of investments besides securities. They look at all the sources of a client's income, what his or her current income needs are, and the client's future expectations.

One of the biggest firms of investment counselors is Scudder, Stevens and Clark, headquartered in Boston. The smallest would have one or two investment counselors and one or two clerical staff. There are advantages to each. A big investment firm has a stable of analysts, a skilled trading department, and an elaborate computer center that can generate a lot of information. Sometimes the problem with a big firm is that it can get in its own way, such as when they ''look at'' a stock. This means the firm considers the stock's pros and cons in depth and may have to buy $40 to $50 million of the stock's total value in order to justify the time and effort put into researching the stock for their clientele. Therefore a big firm can only afford to look at big companies, those with more than a billion dollars in market capitalization; whereas a small firm can afford to look at smaller companies that may be traded so seldom it is difficult to place even a small order to buy. But a small company may be a better investment opportunity just because it is small and can grow more rapidly than a big company. The financial quality, the risk, might be just the same.

Trust officers in banks are often popular among men who believe their wives have little or no financial competence. Banks have an aura of substantiality about them, and for that reason they are frequently named executors of estates. Banks offer several different kinds of investment services. The bank can be investment manager and trustee, hired for that purpose and making the investment decisions. It can also be a custodian officer in charge of simply holding the assets for safekeeping but making no decisions. Many investment counselors use banks in this way if their clients choose not to retain the securities themselves. There is a fee for this service, as for all other bank services. If the bank is trustee, the trust officer is often a lawyer since the bank is responsible for understanding the terms of the trust and complying with them.

Bank administrative officers handle all the detail work. The bank's portfolio manager is someone who manages a portfolio of stocks and bonds and makes decisions about what to sell or buy. He may never see the client. The client sees the investment manager who makes recommendations on the basis of information given by the portfolio manager. Because banks have a tendency to reward people with titles instead of a raise, the individuals managing investment funds in banks change positions rather frequently. You probably wouldn't be able to work with one person over an extended period of time through a bank. So, although banks endure, their personnel do not.

A *security analyst* performs a specialized function. Security analysts look at an individual stock or bond and decide whether that stock or bond should be bought or sold. He or she is dealing with published information about a company, talking with the management of the company, and sometimes writing up reports. In a small investment counseling firm, the members are security analysts, portfolio managers, and client relations people all in one—they wear several hats. In a large bank, there may be an investment officer who deals with clients, a portfolio manager who makes the decisions about what to buy and sell, a separate trader who actually places the order, and a security analyst who investigates the individual securities and makes recommendations to the portfolio manager about what should be bought or sold.

A *stockbroker* acts as an agent to buy or sell securities through the particular brokerage firm he or she works for. Stockbrokers are paid a commission for each transaction. They work in two categories, either directly with individuals and/or with corporations that have pension or profit-sharing plans. The stockbroker advises clients about what to buy or sell; at the same time stockbrokers execute orders carrying out these recommendations. The stockbroker also works with banks and investment counselors, wherein the latter make the investment decisions and stockbroker carries them out.

Some brokerage firms specialize in working with institutions; among these are Goldman, Sachs and Salomon Brothers. Some tend to deal mainly with individuals. There are also discount brokers who handle buy-and-sell orders on which the owner of the security has made her or his own independent decision—they do not make recommendations—for their smaller commission. Some firms, like Merrill Lynch, Pierce, Fenner & Smith, run the gamut from handling small personal accounts to large institutional accounts for large and small banks and investment counselors.

You will want to know the charges for these various services and where you would fit into the sorts of accounts these different financial specialists handle. If the value of your inheritance plus other assets is less than $50,000, not including the house, a good way to handle it might be to invest in a mutual fund, assuming the money came to you from your husband's life insurance or is in a form you do not wish to stay with. A mutual fund, like a money market fund, pools your money with that of many other investors. This large sum is then invested in a diversified portfolio of stocks and bonds managed by the firm.

Look for a good fund. There are literally hundreds of them. *Forbes* magazine lists and ranks them every year—A,B,C,D, and so forth, in declining order. The key thing you want to know about the fund is how it has done over the last *five* years. Any mutual fund could be spectacular for one year because the portfolio manager had a winning streak, say with energy stocks in 1980. What you want to look for is the performance over a longer period, during the ups and downs in the stock market. Try to find one that is B during an up market and B during a down market. That should fit the objectives of a balanced program, a certain amount of income, and a certain amount of growth, which means increase in value. Given these requirements—if a mutual fund is indeed what you want—you should be able to boil the list down to five to six. When you have enough general information, send away for their literature and read it. As soon as you find one you are comfortable with, fill out the form that comes with the prospectus and send it off with a check. If you specifically request it, you can receive a monthly income check from your mutual fund investment; otherwise they send them quarterly or they will reïnvest the income. Once you have made your arrangement with them, you have nothing more to do. There is more discussion and analysis of mutual funds in chapter eight.

A number of women have become stockbrokers in some parts of the country. You might feel more comfortable dealing with another woman at this time. In one investment course, a woman broker described why investments that were very good for her at her particular stage of life would be poor investments for her widowed mother who needed income much more than growth. She seemed especially sensitive to the problems of a woman alone and that can be a real asset in a professional advisor.

Stockbrokers have no particular minimum requirement to open an account, and some are very skilled and conscientious. You should remember that brokers only make money on commissions, which are added to the price of the stocks and bonds they buy and sell for you. A cautionary word that you may hear elsewhere, too, is that you should avoid a broker who has a reputation for "churning," a very nasty word in the business. To explain; the more your stocks are bought and sold, the greater the commissions. So a churner may get you to buy General Motors and sell Ford this year and then buy Ford and sell General Motors next year, just to generate commissions. This is a mere caveat as most brokerage firms have supervisors of individual brokers to keep this from happening. Most experienced brokers are competent and trustworthy people.

Investment counselors are different from stockbrokers in that they have varied minimums in the size of the accounts they handle, anywhere from $200,000 to $500,000 or more.

Their fees are tax deductible. They have no interest in the movement of your investments in or out of the market so long as they are performing well because they make no commissions on these transactions. As stated earlier, their fees are based on a percentage of the total portfolio, so they are growth-oriented.

As with every step you make, consulting your lawyer is always wise, even if the estate has been settled and your phone call generates a bill. Until you feel quite sure of yourself, a consultation may well be worth the price to avoid a mistake that could have serious consequences. You can also feel confident about any recommendations or even introductions the lawyer gave you to professionals. They will naturally want to have your lawyer continue sending them his clients so they have a vested interest in doing a good job for you.

The next chapter discusses bonds, both corporate and government, and other options available for your consideration.

CHAPTER SEVEN

Bonds in the Money World

Consider the choices you have for investing as a smörgasbord of opportunities for putting money to work. There are all kinds of things you can buy, such as stocks and bonds (called by the general term *equities*), gold, silver, paintings, numismatic coins, philatelic stamps and covers, commodity futures, as well as participation in a variety of ventures such as movie productions, and oil or mineral exploration. These latter investments are highly specialized and for the most part do not produce income on a predictable basis. Generally the plan for profit with them is that you buy at one price and sell at a higher one in the best cases. Some of them also have favorable tax advantages.

Real estate is another diversified field. Unless your husband left you real estate investments, also with pleasant tax consequences, you might not want to get into real estate at present, because it can be complicated in a time of tight money. You should become familiar with the field before making any decisions, and even then you want to explore the territory carefully before venturing in. This chapter wil concentrate on bond investing.

First, however, an essential ingredient before investing in anything such as stocks and bonds is to know *why* you are thinking of making the investment in the first place. What do you want? Why, for example, aren't you just putting your money figuratively under the mattress? You *must* know why you are getting ready to contemplate buying stocks and bonds in order to feel confident that this is the right investmen decision for your situation. Do you want tax-free income because you think your tax bracket is too high? Tax-free income is usually less than taxable income. Do you want the maximum current income possible? Do you have a little capital and feel you need more capital growth? Perhaps you don't have enough capital *or* income, so you need more o each. How much risk can you assume? Risk is a euphemism used a lot in the investment world; it means how much you can afford to lose. Are you willing to lose 5%, 10%, or 30% of your money? At what point does your panic button push Remember, it doesn't have to push at the same place for al your money. You can put some in ultraconservative insured savings certificates and take more chances with another chunk of it that seems expendable.

Let's take a hypothetical situation and say you have $100,00 from the life insurance money to invest. You decide you nee to have one-quarter, or $25,000 with a minimum risk so thi amount may go into U.S. Treasuries, not to be confused wit Savings Bonds. You'd like another $25,000 to earn maximur income because you want to use this to supplement your othe income. You study the interest rates of the various mone market funds and high-yield certificates of deposit and choos one. The third $25,000 can go into solid stocks like IBM Eastman Kodak, and General Electric that offer some reliabl growth as well as reliable income. The final $25,000 can permit you the fun of watching how your neighbor is doing with the fabulous idea she's trying to build a business around, or some other appealing and adventurous investment that shows promise of eventual high returns.

You can divide your money up into as many categories as you wish, but you have to know what you are thinking about—what goals you have—for each category. If you don't know your needs and goals, the results will almost certainly be unsatisfactory. What's more, you won't be able to ask sensible questions of your advisors nor understand their answers.

You really have to think about your future thoroughly. "I inherited X dollars from my parents, I have another X amount from my husband's life insurance, and probably the investments we had come to around X thousand." If there is enough, you may want to make some of it work for something your children need or to help educate your grandchildren ten years from now or to take an impecunious friend to Europe for six months. In other words, you need to establish some goals in terms of your needs, beginning with a realistic personal budget of what it will cost to maintain yourself in the style you wish to live.

To illustrate: If you were a twenty-four-year-old profession al, you might say to yourself, "I hope to buy a house by the time I'm thirty. I have a good job. If I invest $2,000, can I hope to have $10,000 in six years for a down payment?"

This would be a plan based on the highest return with a maximum risk. You would not care too much if you lost it because you can expect a promotion and could eventually replace it. On the other hand, in your position you may say to yourself, "I'm 64 and I have $100,000 from my husband's life insurance policy, a couple of small real estate investments, and social security. That's it.'' You can't afford to risk your money so you need safety with maximum income—possibly U.S. government securities.

The most reliable investments are U.S. Treasury bills, notes, and bonds. The difference between them is that the life of a bill is a year or less, a note is from one to five years, and a bond is for more than five years. The U.S. Treasury is the most credit-worthy organization in the world today; therefore it is going to pay the least interest because the likelihood of the treasury going bankrupt is remote—the risk is low.

U.S. Treasury issues are an example of the most safety, yielding the least cash income to you. Next come government-affiliated agencies like the Federal Home Loan Bank, the Farm Credit Loan Bank, Federal National Mortgage Association, and a whole lot of other organizations that are connected with the government and borrow under the government's guarantee. These are usually issued as bonds and are slightly less reliable than the treasury itself, so you will get slightly more interest.

What is a bond? The simplest thing in the world. It is nothing but an IOU. A bond is a contract between a borrower and a lender. You read or hear that bonds are said to be ''at par.'' In this case par has nothing to do with golf. It is one of those esoteric words of the financial world, meaning the value the bond had when it was originally issued.

Most of the federal government-affiliated bonds including Treasuries—though not all—are free of *state* income taxes; they are non-taxable on your state income tax return, though interest on such securities is fully taxable by the Internal Revenue Service, at the *federal* level.

Currently popular are the municipal IOUs. Years ago, the federal government was anxious that we lend our money to government entities other than at the federal level to help finance the establishment of the ''alabaster cities'' of ''America the Beautiful.'' Municipal bonds include funding for housing, schools, ports, airports, and the maintenance of nearly everything—bridges, roads, water and sewer systems. In order to make such bonds attractive to the public, the federal government said that it would not tax any interest paid by local governments. The state of Wisconsin, for example, also followed up, guaranteeing that municipal bonds would be free of state taxes also. Therefore, if you want to be completely tax free, you lend to entities in the state where you live, only. But there may be reasons you don't want to do that—your own state may not be a good credit risk. Some cities are also not good credit risks. A number of them have been having a rocky time of it lately. You'll want to investigate the ins and outs of these various options by discussing them with professionals.

If you paid a visit to the brokerage house or have been to a bank trust office or an investment advisory firm, the impact of it may have made you feel inferior and stupid. The people you talked to were so competent and bright, it may have seemed there could be no argument with what they said. That is nonsense. The people you met are no brighter than you, some of them considerably less so. They just have more experience with a specialty you don't know much about yet, and sometimes it appears as though they want to keep it that way so that the somewhat mysterious services they offer seem more valuable. Ignorant, apprehensive *you* may have money to invest, and they want to take care of it for you—for a fee—but a week's seminar on demystifying the world of money is often not included. Remember you are the client and the boss. Don't allow yourself to be rushed into anything, and ask about any term or concept that puzzles you.

For some reason, bonds seem more puzzling than stocks to many people. As mentioned, bonds are simply IOUs. For example, say I borrow $1,000 from you and agree to pay you back in three years, or two or one. You'll get your money back on the date we agreed on. And in the meantime, I agree to pay you 10% interest. You write out the IOU note, and I pay you *rent* for the use of your money during the time and in the amount we agreed on. When you think of interest as rent, it's a very simple concept. For lending money to anyone you get back a return based on three things. Visualize, if you will, a circle divided into three parts. (See illustration, page 111.) The size of each part depends on how the whole is divided up. One of the parts is safety, which reflects the credit worthiness of whoever borrows the money. Another is *cash*, or return, or *interest*. The third is the *time* or speed with which you regain control of the money you lent—termed liquidity. If you get more of one of the three ingredients, you will get less of the others.

For example, if you lend money to a not very reliable borrower, you're going to get a higher than usual rate of interest, and the principal, or amount you lent, will be repaid in a shorter time. Your industrious sister may ask you to lend her $1,000 so she can avoid paying interest to a finance company to complete the purchase of a new car. You will probably agree and lend her the money at 8% for as long as she wanted. This is a lower rate than the finance company or the bank would charge her because you know she will pay you back as soon as she can. But if your profligate nephew wanted the same amount of money for the purchase of a motorcycle to replace the one he had just totally demolished, which was underinsured, you might say, "Yes, but I want it back in six months and it will be at 15%." Your different attitude toward the two borrowers depends on your estimate of their credit ratings.

A family situation is really no different from a corporate situation. It is all very logical. The more suspect a person's credit rating is, the more nervous you are going to be, the more time limits you're going to set up, and the more rent for your money you are going to charge.

If you are lending to IBM, which has a triple A rating (AAA)—the best according to Standard and Poor's—you can relax. On the other hand, if your neighbor with her struggling young company wants a loan, it's a very different matter. You would lend the money to IBM for less interest and a longer time than to your neighbor, whom you would be visiting every morning to inquire how her company is coming along. So the return goes—lots of safety, less return of cash and lots of liquidity; *or* little safety, little liquidity, lots of cash. These things balance out in most loan transactions.

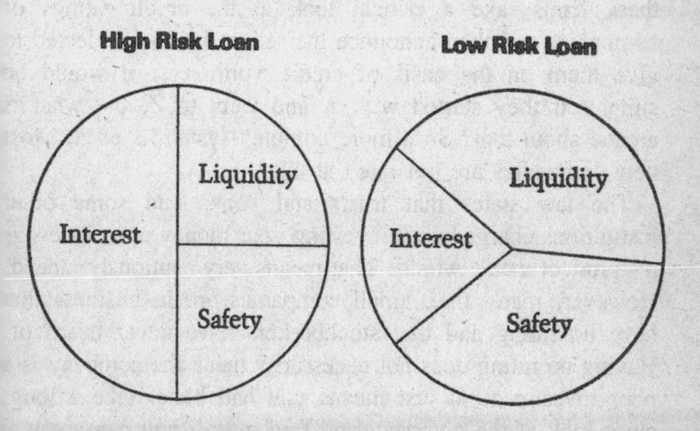

An additional factor is the impact of inflation during the life of the loan. If you think there is going to be a 10% rate averaged over the years you are lending money, you want to be able to buy as much with the $1,000 you will get back in ten years as you can buy with it now. To do this, you will charge $100 a year for the 10% inflation you expect over the time period, and then 2% on top of that for profit for a rate of 12%.

Not very "high finance," is it? That's what is so encouraging about the basics of money management—how simple the things are that financiers have been doing all these years. They just dress it up in a vocabulary only the initiated can understand. The underlying ideas and even the math are elementary. What you want is your money back with its original buying power plus a reasonable profit, and that's what bonds are all about.

If you are looking for a taxable bond, which would pay more interest than tax-free ones, you think of lending your money to corporations. Some corporate bonds are rated by two outfits—Standard & Poor's and Moody's. The people at these firms take a critical look at the credit ratings of companies and then announce the rating they have elected to give them on the basis of credit worthiness. It would be simpler if they started with A and went to Z, but what is arcane about that? So a more complex system is used. Most new companies are not rated at all.

The law states that trusts and banks and some other institutions charged with investing your money must invest as a "prudent man" would. That means very cautiously indeed. However, many fine, small companies are in business that have no rating and that stockbrokers have never heard of. Having no rating does not necessarily mean the company is a poor investment; it just means you had better take a long, close look at the company and find out all you can about it before you invest. Banks and trust companies are not allowed to invest in anything that doesn't have a grade A rating. However, there is one problem with even excellent small companies that have no rating. Since they borrow relatively small amounts of money, you may have a harder time selling their bonds than you otherwise would when you need the cash.

It is hard to pinpoint the number of small companies that

employ less than two hundred people, yet about 95% of the companies in this country are small. The New York Stock Exchange lists about 1,650 companies, and about the same number are carried on the American Stock Exchange and the Over-the-Counter markets combined, so we are talking about only 3,200 companies out of the thousands that exist.

If a company is going to float a big bond issue, say $25 to $50 million, they will want to have the issue rated because the higher the rating, as the circle diagram showed earlier, the less rent they will have to pay for the money, since a high rating should give you top security. Companies are very anxious to have a rating, and once they have it, they are very anxious to have their rating upgraded. Every now and then you will read something like this in the financial pages. "Franklin County suffers disaster—rating falls from A to A−." That may not seem like much of a fall, but it can mean that Franklin County, borrowing $10,000,000 at 8% instead of 7¾% for thirty years, will have to pay a difference of $750,000 more in interest over the life of the loan. That is, the taxpayers will have to pay it.

Let's study, as an example, a portfolio that includes $5,000 Braintree, Massachusetts, general obligation bonds, $20,000 Massachusetts State general obligation bonds, $15,000 Massachusetts State Port Authority revenues. You can see the owner probably lived in and liked Massachusetts. Start with the $15,000 Massachusetts Port Authority Revenue, labeled JJI, 5.70, 7/1/93. Let's go over it precisely. 15,000—this person owns 15 one-thousand dollar bonds. The State of Massachusetts borrowed the money for the Port Authority. It is to be paid back by revenues gathered by the Port Authority; that is ships coming into the harbor, docking to load and unload, which have to pay fees. JJI means that the interest on the bonds has to be paid on January 1 and July 1, since bonds pay twice a year, every six months. Now to figure out how much it will be—look at 5.70—that means 5.7%. Each bond therefore will pay $57.00 a year. So every six months, on each bond, the owner will get $28.50. Multiply that by 15, since there are 15 bonds, and $427.50 will be paid to that individual twice a year, or $855.00 a year.

A "normal" lot of bonds is 100, and bonds usually come in $1,000 lots. But few of us have $100,000 to put down in one investment; an easier purchase is to buy them in increments of 5. More people are going to want to buy them from you later on in lots of 5, 10, 15, or 20 bonds rather than 2, 3 or 4 bonds, which won't "fit" into any pension plan, bank, or mutual fund's program. Keep your bond purchases in increments of 5; that way you can sell them for more or buy them for less because they are a nice, neat commonly traded number. Like stocks, bonds are bought and sold through a brokerage firm.

Though the interest rates on bonds do not change during the life of the bond, the price at which they are bought and sold does change. For example, you may want to cash in a bond. Time has gone by, money has become a lot more plentiful (this example is *very* hypothetical), and the interest rate on money, or rent, has dropped from 10% a year to 5% a year. You tell your potential buyer that your IOU is for $5,000 and is paying 10% or $500 a year. Have you a guess about what you could sell it for? The current rate is 5%, or $250 a year income for $5,000 lent. Because money is cheap and the interest rates have fallen, you can expect to sell your bond for $10,000. Because current money is being lent at 5% and you lent it at 10%, the value of your IOU has risen so that the amount of its interest becomes comparable to the interest rate currently charged. This *was* very hypothetical.

The *length of time* of the loan is fixed and can't be changed. It is due on the date stipulated. The amount of the loan, $5,000, is fixed and can't be changed. There is only one variable and that is the *value* of the loan. The capital, or market value, of the loan rises and falls, adjusting the return you are getting to today's rate of return. Thus the value has risen to $10,000 because the return you are getting is 5% of that, not 5% of $5,000. The $10,000 figure at the new rate, 5%, produces the same amount, $500, as you were getting at the old 10% rate on $5,000.

Let's reverse our example and assume that interest rates went up. Suppose you lent the money at 10% and the interest rates went up to 20%, which *has* happened. Under those circumstances, when you try to sell your IOU, you would be offered $2,500 for your $5,000 note. It would be nice if bonds always sold at what was paid for them, but this is seldom the case. Every day, every IOU you have lent goes up or down as the value of your rent changes vis-à-vis the current market. The price of bonds at any given time is set by the money rates, all bonds from AAA on down. When money, or interest rates go *down*, bond prices rise, because it costs less to buy more principal amount of any given issue. When interest rates go *up*, bond prices fall because it costs more to buy more principal amount of an issue. Understanding this relationship is fundamental to understanding the importance of money rates generally.

There is something else interesting about bonds; they rise and fall in unison, by categories. For example, the value of a 10% AA bond coming due in 1995 will go up or down along with all other 10% AAs of 1995. They all go up or down together.

To review: If you have a $1,000 IOU paying 5% or $50 and the rent goes up to 10%, the capital value of the IOU would drop to the point where $50 becomes 10%—no longer 5%—of the capital value. In other words, the capital value would drop from $1,000 to $500 because $50 is 10% of $500.

The ingredients of a bond, then, are the maturity date (the date when you will be paid back), the amount of rent or interest to be paid (called the interest rate), and the credit rating of the borrower. Tax free bonds don't pay as much as corporate bonds because the fact that you will pay no tax on the income from them is an extra benefit to you.

If you have a choice between the State of Massachusetts Port Authority revenue bonds paying 5.7% and American Tel & Tel bonds for the same length of time paying 12%, how do you decide which you want? If you are in a 50% tax bracket, 50% of AT&T's interest at 12% is going to be taken away from you by the IRS. That would still leave you more than you would be getting from the Massachusetts bonds because you would keep 6% instead of 5.7%. Some states demand little or no income tax, some a lot. So where you live and what income tax bracket you are in become factors to consider in what sort of bonds you buy.

Naturally, you will buy bonds that enable you to keep the largest part of the interest they pay. It's purely selfish—how to get the most for the least. That should be what you are figuring out all the time. Do you get it from a bond, a stock, a house, or some old coins? Where do you put your money so that the return will be greatest, and what kind of risk can you accept in so doing?

How about keeping a bond to maturity? Are there any disadvantages in that? You might want to sell all your bonds for some pressing reason, and you might be forced to take a tremendous loss on them if interest rates went up after you bought them. If you could keep them to maturity date, you know you will be repaid your original investment. There are as many reasons for selling bonds as there are for holding them. What is guiding you all the time is pure, unadulterated self-interest. This is a situation where loyalty to a company or sentiment attached to an investment is both unwise and misplaced. An investment is not a keepsake nor a family heirloom, and nothing is quite as soulless as a corporation. Enlightened self-interest is the name of the game, always with emphasis on the word *enlightened*. You would never get a "thank you" note from the chairman of the board of a corporation for holding its bonds while the corporation went bankrupt.

Unless a bond is listed on the *Wall Street Journal* bond page, it is not easy to check the current price. Most local newspapers do not carry bond prices. If you own some you can't find in the *Journal*, you have to call a broker or investment counselor giving this information: "I have Niagara Mohawk Power 7¾s of '02, (meaning the year 2002). What are they selling at?" You always give the name of the borrower, the amount of the rent, and the date of maturity. If you don't have these three facts, they can't help you because there are other Niagara Mohawk Powers at 7⅝ of '03—you have to be exact. To help you do your own research, Standard & Poor's *Bond Guide* is as useful in the bond field as is the *Stock Guide* for common stocks.

There are also two sorts of bond funds. You might consider them if you don't want to put all your eggs in one basket. If you decide you don't want to lend it all to Niagara Mohawk, or AT&T or the water district of the city you live in, you have a choice of bond funds or corporate bonds, which are taxable, and bond funds that are not taxable. They work approximately the same way. The fund managers buy $40 million worth of IOUs, bonds, put them all together and figure out how much income is due from the $40 million, and then they figure out what the overall interest rate is. That done, they announce a new series paying 8.05%, tax free. What you buy is a slice of this batch of bonds. Perhaps the minimum will be $5,000. Whatever you buy pays you the announced interest rate, and normally the bonds are not paid back for 15 to 20 years. This is called a unit trust. It is not managed. The company buys the collection of bonds and that's that. They go into a safe deposit box somewhere until maturity.

The situation is different in a mutual fund for municipal (tax-free) bonds or corporate bonds (taxable.) They are being bought and sold regularly because new money comes into the funds all the time. Mutual funds are constantly adding to or subtracting from their portfolio, so the interest rate changes incessantly.

There is a lot to choose from, so you need to know what you want and why you want it. A general rule is that if you are in a 30% or below income tax bracket—and your accountant can tell you if you don't know—you are better off with taxable bonds. Bonds, once more, are simply loans—short term, medium term, or long term.

You buy the sort that fit your particular needs when you know what they are. Do you need the highest possible income with no tax worries? Do you plan to help your grandchildren through college which the oldest will be entering in ten years? If you want to help your grandchildren with college, you should probably buy bonds heavily discounted today that will mature in the right years to follow their educational careers. You would get a return on your capital as the years roll by and have a nice capital gain at the right time when the bonds pay off at face value. A *capital gain* is often referred to warmly by investors. If a capital gain is long-term, the difference between what you paid and the higher price you sell at (the gain), will be taxed at a significantly *lower* rate than ordinary income. It's a nice way to make money cheaply. Capital gain is most often associated with the increase in value of real estate, but it is commonly associated with stocks and bonds as well.

Here's another option for you. If you look over the New York Bond Exchange page, you will notice an entry like this—K-mart 6s 99 *cv*. The *cv* means convertible subordinated debenture. Here, specifically, it means K-mart 6%, 1999 *convertible subordinated debentures*. In the case of bankruptcy, the CVs would be honored after bonds but before stocks. They are bonds, but they rank below the original bonds. What about the convertible feature? Since they are bonds, you have some cash coming, some safety coming, and liquidity, the ability to get hold of your money. And you have a fourth category—you have the ability to convert them into the company's stock when you want to. As Sylvia Porter says, "These are bonds that give the owner the extra privilege of converting into a certain number of shares of common stock of the same corporation." CVs have lower "downside" risk and about the same "upside" potential as the underlying common stock. Though they yield less than straight bonds, there is a chance of making an additional profit if the company's stock goes up.

Everything in the stock market has a monetary value. When the president of the company resigns, he can find out exactly how important he was to that company. If the company's stock doesn't move at all, he might feel somewhat depressed. He apparently didn't make any difference to its fortunes.

You probably understand now that money is bought just like carrots or houses or cars. When there is a lot of it around, it's cheap. When there's just a little around, it becomes expensive. Like anything else you buy, it's a commodity. You have to stop thinking of money only as something to buy things *with*, because it in itself is a *thing* that is bought and sold. When you figure out what you want your money to do, you will be able to decide exactly what sort of investments you need.

The next chapter may help you make this decision.

CHAPTER EIGHT

Investing Should Be an Informed Decision

Perhaps you are feeling somewhat overwhelmed by this discussion of stocks and bonds and their uses. Let's look at some other ways of making money work to your advantage.

Until interest rates went out of sight, making the cost of borrowing money very expensive, real estate was the glamorous attraction to many investors. And a lot of investors did very well with it for a time. Some still do. As of this writing, the real estate field isn't too inviting for the cautious investor who wants liquidity. The property should have a good track record, such as an apartment house with a good occupancy rate over several years in an area that is improving, not deteriorating. Perhaps an early investor wants to sell his piece or a portion of it. If you don't understand how real estate investments work, get someone who does to look over the performance record of anything you consider buying.

Real estate has one big attraction as an investment—it provides a good way to reduce your income taxes due to some generous provisions Congress has written into the tax codes over the years. The recurrent emergence of the "flat tax" notion must make real estate investors' blood turn to ice water at the possibility of losing those attractive benefits. A flat tax would be a fixed percentage tax on income from all sources—with no deductions whatever.

The monetary advantage of owning real property is that while it presumably grows in value, you can deduct a lot of the annual income from it because, according to the tax code, the building is depreciating. The value in terms of the real estate market may be going up or appreciating, but the tax writers perceive the building as wearing out and therefore depreciating at the same time. Following the proper tables, you can deduct a certain amount called depreciation from your income. Other expenses can be added to your deductions, too: the costs of maintaining the property, the taxes, repairs, redecorations between tenants and so on, and any cost to you of supervision or management of the property. Still a further deduction can be added to this—that is, subtracted from your income for tax purposes. The amount of interest paid on the mortgage is tax deductible. The interest, compared to repayment of principal, declines annually until it finally becomes zero at the time the loan is paid off.

If the mortgage loan is new or refinanced, the amount of interest compared to principal in the amount of monthly payments is very large in the early years of a loan. For example, on a monthly mortgage payment of $1,300, $1,000 or more may be payment of interest in the early years of the loan, which means you can deduct $12,000 yearly in interest payments from your income.

With high interest rates it is hard to derive personal income from real estate, even though rents may be raised as high as the traffic will bear. In other words, you may have to pay out more in monthly payments than you can get back in rent. This creates a situation called negative cash flow, as you pay the bank that holds the mortgage more money than the property produces. Some people need a negative cash flow, but it is unlikely that you do.

Inflationary times are a boon to real estate partnerships because they expect to sell a property for far more than it cost and enjoy the tax benefits until a suitable buyer is found. Depending on your point of view of the future inflation picture and your need for personal income, you may or may not regard a real estate investment with enthusiasm. In any case, each real estate deal is different, with its own characteristics and advantages. These are often difficult for a novice to assess. Probably the safest and most productive investment in today's market is a duplex or fourplex residence where the owner occupies one of the units and then gets the tax benefits of a landlord from the rentals. This could be a good investment provided the rents carry enough of the mortgage payments.

If you are interested in real estate investing, find a realtor you can trust to lead you through the maze. Then check out any specific plan to purchase with a disinterested but educated third party, such as the attorney who handled the probate of your husband's estate. It will be worth paying his fee to avoid getting in over your head. Although real estate investment has many inherent tax savings, it is a field requiring expert knowledge. Many people take a course or two in real estate investments before they start looking at properties.

As for precious gems, numismatic coins, philatelic stamps and covers, works of art, gold and silver, oriental rugs, movie productions and oil drilling ventures, unless you are an expert in the particular field, stay away until you become knowledgeable or are feeling very rich, can afford the high risk, don't care about income, and want the excitement of gambling.

Unless you have a particular interest in the specialty investments, you will probably want to stick with the more ordinary means of investing. But you may well wonder how, among the more conventional investments of stocks and bonds, you can tell which stock would be a good one for you to buy. How can you tell one from another? Which will serve your interest and which will not? I have already stressed the importance of your input. You need to know what your interests and goals are before you can make sensible choices. But you also need an understanding of the securities market in general.

The Dow Jones average that you hear about on the radio daily is the average of thirty of the biggest companies in the United States. If you don't know which they are, just start with the word *General*—General Electric, General Motors, General Foods—huge companies. The relation of their price per share to the amount that they earn per share, their *P/E* (price earnings ratio), is roughly 8½ to 1. These companies also yield an average rate of 5%. Needless to say, these figures do not represent any one company: They are an average. But let's review it because it is central to our discussion.

I've already mentioned the price-earnings ratio. Earnings are what is left over after the cost of producing whatever they produce is added up. Assume a million shares of the company are held by the public—this is called having a million shares outstanding. When you buy a stock, it is very different from when you buy a bond. When you buy a bond, you've lent some company some money. When you buy a stock, it's somewhat like buying a house or a car or a dress: You are affected by whatever happens to that object. It could be the car conks out and dies, or the house is "eminent-domained," which means the state takes it over for public use, usually but not always with compensation. It could turn out that you bought a fine car, but they cut off the assembly line, making the car a museum piece valued at eight times what you paid for it. Whatever happens to this possession of yours happens to you. It's the same way with stocks. If the company you own shares in suddenly invents a cure for the common cold in pill form, the company's stock is going to take off, and you will be able to take all your favorite relatives on a world cruise. If, on the other hand, the entire laboratory blows up, the opposite happens to the stock and to you. You lose out.

So, let's say a million shares are out, and the company earns a million dollars; then one dollar's worth of earnings accrues to each share. The stock is selling for $10 a share, making the relationship of the price of the stock to the earnings per share, 10 to 1. This is the price-earnings ratio or the P/E. It's listed in the newspaper every day in one of the columns after the stock designation. The average relationship of the price to the earnings of the thirty big Dow Jones stocks is 8% to 1. The Dow Jones average rise in a stock is about 5% a year, and the stocks pay dividends of roughly 5% of the price of the stock. Obviously the story of Eastman Kodak is very different from General Foods and even more different from General Motors. There are tremendous variations among these stocks, but the Dow Jones figures represent the average and that can give you a working guideline.

The significance of the P/E, the price of the stock divided by the earnings per share, is how the P/E of one company compares with that of other companies within the same industry or with the Dow Jones stocks. (Remember the P/E is *earnings* per share, not *dividends* per share. The dividends depend on how the company's board of directors decide to spread the earnings or profits.) If the P/E ratio gets higher than the ratio of the industry, the possibility is that the price of the stock will drop. If you have a company with a P/E lower than the average in the industry, the possibility is the price will rise. This is a general rule to which exceptions certainly exist. For example, people are often willing to pay more for a stock in a company that is growing fast. It is likely to be ploughing back all the profits into research and development, new plant, and so on. Stockholders in such ventures are buying into the future, and the further into the future they are buying, the more chance there is for error; this is a high-risk situation. In financial circles you hear about the projections, what the company is supposed to earn, per share, next year, hopefully made by knowledgeable people. But these are only prophecies—crystal ball readings. They are worth keeping in mind, of course, but like everything else to do with the stock market, and life in general, projections are subject to change without notice. If the crystal ball is clear you can make a lot of money. If wrong, you won't.

You have to consider the risks and your own situation before you go into something glamorous that a broker may be pushing hard. You have to know how much risk you can afford to accept and how much suspense you can stand. Can you afford to lose half your investment in something? You could do this very easily. All a company has to do is earn $1.00 or $1.25 until the rumor goes out that the principal mainstay of the business is drying out in a sanatorium upstate somewhere and may not be back; then everything changes. Instead of looking at a company with a ten-year record of growing earnings, you're looking at a company that is without its chief engineer who was its spark plug; it is now a very dull company indeed. Suddenly you may have a stock worth $5 that you paid $25 for.

The figures relating to a stock vary all day long, every day. One woman who has been a broker for many years said she could recall only one stock that remained entirely logical during her years in the business. It was the Washington Real Estate Trust. Ten or fifteen years ago it could be bought for $10 a share, and it paid an $.80 dividend. The P/E remained the same and the yield was the same over the years, though the price rose to $48 a share and the dividend grew accordingly. Only this one stock of the thousands traded daily follows a logical progression in her experience. The lesson is that logic may play a part in the stock market, but it doesn't rule its fluctuations. Stocks are affected by many situations and events. They can run in fads, which adds another unknown and uncontrollable factor to a volatile scene. Why then invest in stocks if there are so many unknowns?

People invest in the bond market for conservation of capital and steady income. People go into the stock market for capital gains and increasing income. When you go into the stock market, you risk your capital. In the bond market you have no capital risk if you hold on from start to finish, though the finish may be a long way off and inflation may erode its buying power. You may risk buying power, meantime, because the market value of the bonds may go down and because the interest is fixed and will not rise with inflation, but if you hold your bonds to maturity, you are not risking capital, only the worth of the dollars.

In uncertain times you may say to yourself, "I must have this much capital back and I must be able to rely on this much income." That means bonds. On the other hand, if you are scared to death of inflation while living on a fixed income and you need to have more revenue, you will look at stocks. But you should be aware that a severe recession can erode the earnings of certain susceptible industries, and dividends can be reduced or omitted altogether for a period.

Let's look at a sample portfolio a widow received. This is how the holdings were arranged when she inherited them: there was Air Products, selling at seven times earnings and yielding 2.7%. Not very much. There was British Petroleum, paying 8% with a P/E of 5, and several others that paid nothing. Except for a convertible debenture and bonds, and the British Petroleum, this portfolio was designed for capital gains. That means the buyer was expecting to cash in the stocks after they had risen to a satisfactory point and pay a tax on that revenue at a lower rate than the regular income tax. Her husband and his investment adviser had set it up that way because her husband could rely on his earnings for income. Now, as a widow, she needed income more than capital growth—she was more concerned about her own future than leaving large sums to her heirs. So she moved into stocks that offered her income and some growth in a proportion suited to her needs, always maintaining some funds in more dependable securities.

Dividends go up and down with a company's earnings, and they have little relation to the price of the stock. They only go up or down with the profits. Most companies that have been in business for a reasonable length of time have a percentage of profit they historically pay out. People who need to be cautious—especially elderly ones—look for "safe" stocks because they realize the necessity for increasing income to maintain their buying power, so long as inflation runs through the economy like an underground river. The only reliable way to increase income in the stock market is to buy into a company that has a solid history of regularly increasing its dividend. This in turn can only come from a company pattern of regularly earning more money. As mentioned earlier, companies are extremely reluctant to lower their dividend because it will result in bad publicity; they will only do so under drastic circumstances. If income is important to you, then the dividend is important to you. Normally, a company won't start out paying a dividend, but when it begins paying even a few cents a quarter, the company directors will do almost anything to keep on giving you those few cents.

When you have your money needs clearly in mind, you can start toward investment decision. If you require maximum income right now, today, then you will be looking for a company that pays 75% of its earnings and has done this on a regular basis. You can look for such a company in the *Stock Guide*, where you can check its history and see for yourself. Such a company, paying out such a large percent of its profits, is not going to grow very fast.

The growth of some companies is controlled by external factors. Utilities, like Commonwealth Edison, aren't allowed to raise the rates they charge their customers unless the regulatory commission of the state they are in says they can, so they tend to stay the same size and pay high dividends. Other companies traditionally do not expand and therefore return the profits of the company to the shareholders in generous amounts. These companies also will not grow, which means your capital will not increase. The reason you should invest in them is for the current return—today. It isn't possible to generalize about such companies, but those less sensitive to the marketplace forces tend to be more stable in performance.

However, if you are as interested in tomorrow as today, then you may be willing to take less return in exchange for more growth; this decision depends on the particulars of your circumstances. As the return gets bigger, the growth gets smaller—almost a rule of thumb. If you get a 13% dividend yield on your investment, you don't expect the company to grow more than 1% or 2% a year. This was almost a portrait of AT&T before it was dismembered. It sold for about six times earnings, grew about 5% a year, paid 10% dividends, and performed like that for a very long time. When it raised its dividend from $1.25 per share per quarter to $1.35 per share per quarter it made a lot of difference to a lot of people all over the United States who chose that company because they considered it utterly reliable as a dividend payer. You've probably noticed that there are several long distance phone companies now, and local department stores are selling telephones. So even this old reliable has changed.

The basic message of this passage is that when you invest in the stock market, you can't afford to play Rip van Winkle and just forget about it, unless someone in whom you have full confidence is watching it for you.

To give you a feeling of what the P/E ratio can indicate, let's look at some companies with widely different P/Es on which information has been gathered. You know that to get the price-earnings ratio, you divide the price of the stock by the earnings per share of the company. For example, $1 million earned applied to one million shares outstanding is $1 earned per share. If that stock sells for $10, you have a P/E of 10 to 1, the relationship of price to earnings. This tells you a lot about the stock. The Dow Jones average has a P/E of 8½. The stocks in the Dow Jones have an average growth of 5%, and a return on capital, or dividend, of 5%. The Dow Jones is cited as a yardstick because it is an average of thirty of the largest companies in the country.

A recent public opinion poll asked people what they thought most companies made, and the answer was a profit margin of 44%. If that were true, it would be the biggest bonanza ever. Business obviously hasn't been telling its story very well.

First we'll look at a company called Tenneco, a conglomerate of oil, natural gas, farm equipment, construction, and insurance. The P/E is 8; the price of the stock is eight times what each share earned. The dividend is $2.80, which is a yield of 7%. It shows a Standard & Poor's of A+. Standard & Poor's get out a separate sheet on the 3,200 or so companies listed on the New York Stock Exchange and the American Stock Exchange. More than 11,000 companies are listed in the *Guide*.

If you hear about a company at a dinner party, a "hot tip of the week" sort of thing that interests you, don't call your advisor and say, "I heard about Pacific Palisades, Inc., listed on the Toronto Exchange.'' Ask, instead, for the S&P sheet on the company. You can't expect your advisor to research every company you pick up a rumor about. A broker, for instance, has between 200 and 1,000 clients, depending on the kind of business he or she does, and hasn't time to research all your discoveries. Research them yourself so you will know more about them in the first place.

You should understand that although Standard & Poor's is accurate and current, it doesn't come right out and tell you that one thing is a roaring ''buy'' or that something else is an obvious ''sell.'' The publishers let the data speak for themselves. The reason is that millions of people all over the country read these sheets, and Standard & Poor's doesn't want to be responsible for people rushing into their broker with a buy or sell order based on their recommendations. The factual data are accurate; from there, you are on your own. The opinion part of their stock analysis is likely to be rather vague.

On the S&P sheet (see illustration pages), it says that Tenneco is a diversified company deriving more than two-thirds of its operations from integrated oil and natural gas pipeline operations, and this is balanced mainly by construction equipment and farm machinery, shipbuilding, chemicals, and automobile components. Extension of the long-term earnings is expected, helped in recent years by higher prices and expanded domestic production in oil and gas.

Tenneco has been approximating the Dow Jones average and selling at eight times earnings; it is close to the Dow on all counts. What you see here is a large company that is stable and predictable too. On the next page, the first thing you look at is whether they sold more each year than they did the year before. So you look for the years and the revenues under income data; you see that almost every year the revenues rise and operating income rises. Next it shows percentage of operating income to revenues; that is the margin of profit. It stayed pretty steady between 14% and 17%, with some variations. Capital expenditures we won't bother with and depreciation we won't bother with, but the next-to-last column is net income, and that has been going up every year. Each column that should be going up, *is* going up.

Then you notice a listing under per share data. That is the book value, or more or less what you would have if the company were sold and all the assets were distributed. The book value goes up every year. Next there is earnings per share. It goes from $4.08 in 1974 to $5.90 in 1982. This is a good, steady increase. Then you see dividends. They go from $1.52 in 1974 to $2.74 in 1983; they nearly doubled. The company's growth was faster than the rate of inflation; the dollar did not drop 100% during those years. People who must live solely on income from investments are interested in finding companies like this whose earnings grow on a predictable basis and whose dividends grow also.

You've read here several times that dividends are paid out of a company's earnings. Therefore the dividend can't go up unless the earnings go up, and companies generally pay out about the same percentage of earnings each year. Because the earnings are rising, the dividends are rising. In recession years, the earnings may either be flat or go down, though as mentioned earlier, most companies do everything possible to sustain the dividend.

That is why a lot of people living off dividends in an inflationary period are not so badly pinched by the decreasing purchasing power of the dollar. The price of their stock may have dropped, in fact the payout ratio went down in those years, but the dividend was going up—a benefit of not being on a fixed income. Tenneco is a conservative company; in 1974, it was plowing 61% of its earnings back into the

2201

Tenneco Inc.

Income Data (Million $)

Year Ended Dec. 31	Revs.	Oper. Inc.	% Oper. Inc. of Revs.	Cap. Exp.	Depr.	Int. Exp.	Net Bef. Taxes	Eff. Tax Rate	Net Inc.	% Net Inc. of Revs.
[1]1984	14,890	2,560	17.2%	1,748	1,133	915	[2] 912	30.8%	631	4.2%
1983	14,449	2,326	16.1%	1,609	980	856	[2]1,041	31.2%	716	5.0%
[3]1982	14,979	2,568	17.1%	2,103	1,035	939	[2]1,202	30.1%	840	5.6%
[1]1981	15,462	2,504	16.2%	2,359	865	896	[2]1,271	36.0%	813	5.3%
[1]1980	13,226	1,967	14.9%	1,825	633	[3]617	[2]1,121	35.2%	726	5.5%
[1]1979	11,209	1,794	16.0%	1,477	564	492	[2] 898	36.2%	[3]571	5.1%
[1]1978	8,762	1,462	16.7%	1,008	449	345	[2] 807	42.0%	466	5.3%
[1]1977	7,440	1,374	18.5%	714	398	257	[2] 807	46.7%	427	5.7%
1976	6,423	1,175	18.3%	613	355	234	[2] 674	42.6%	384	6.0%
1975	5,630	1,051	18.7%	545	337	238	[2] 603	42.5%	343	6.1%

Balance Sheet Data (Million $)

Dec. 31	Cash	——Current—— Assets	Liab.	Ratio	Total Assets	Ret. on Assets	Long Term Debt	Common Equity	Total Cap.	% LT Debt of Cap.	Ret. on Equity
1984	73	3,383	3,365	1.0	18,205	3.4%	5,069	6,150	14,498	35.0%	9.3%
1983	167	4,016	3,822	1.1	17,994	4.0%	5,137	5,819	13,872	37.0%	11.5%
1982	45	4,192	3,982	1.1	17,378	4.8%	5,032	5,471	13,069	38.5%	14.4%
1981	76	4,494	4,146	1.1	16,808	5.1%	5,089	5,042	12,303	41.4%	15.6%
1980	74	3,991	3,532	1.1	13,853	5.4%	4,161	4,160	9,919	41.9%	17.1%
1979	117	3,945	3,662	1.1	11,631	5.1%	3,173	3,341	7,675	41.3%	16.2%
1978	121	3,388	2,657	1.3	10,134	5.0%	3,067	3,074	7,254	42.3%	14.6%
1977	82	2,678	2,111	1.3	8,278	5.3%	2,391	2,798	5,940	40.3%	15.2%
1976	125	2,165	1,624	1.3	7,177	5.4%	2,318	2,318	5,335	43.4%	16.4%
1975	123	1,853	1,364	1.4	6,584	5.0%	2,280	1,940	4,998	45.6%	17.0%

Data as orig. reptd. 1. Reflects merger or acquisition. 2. Incl. equity in earns. of nonconsol. subs. 3. Excl. discontinued opers.

Business Summary

Contributions to revenues (before elimination of intergroup sales) and operating income of this diversified energy company in 1984 were:

	Revs.	Profits
Oil expl. & prod.	10%	55%
Pipelines	28%	26%
Oil processing & marketing, & chemicals	18%	−14%
Manufacturing	31%	16%
*Life insurance	---	6%
Fiber, food, land & other	13%	12%

*Equity in earnings of unconsolidated subsidiaries included on an after-tax basis.

Oil exploration and production operations are conducted through Tenneco Oil. Proved reserves at December 31, 1984 totaled 369 million barrels of oil and liquids and 3,545 Bcf of natural gas.

Tennessee Gas Transmission and Tenngasco transport natural gas over 17,700 miles of pipeline through the Appalachian area, the Eastern Seaboard, New England, the Upper Midwest and the Texas Gulf Coast. Gas sales and transportation volumes in 1984 were 2,020 Bcf, versus 1,669 Bcf a year earlier.

TGT formed Tenngasco Exchange Corp. in 1984 to participate in natural gas spot markets.

Other subsidiaries include J. I. Case, Walker Manufacturing, Monroe Auto Equipment, and Newport News Shipbuilding.

Dividend Data

Dividends have been paid since 1948. A dividend reinvestment plan is available.

Amt. of Divd. $	Date Decl.	Ex-divd. Date	Stock of Record	Payment Date
0.73	Oct. 30	Nov. 1	Nov. 8	Dec. 11'84
0.73	Jan. 22	Feb. 4	Feb. 8	Mar. 12'85
0.73	Apr. 26	May 6	May 10	Jun. 11'85
0.73	Jul. 23	Aug. 5	Aug. 9	Sep. 10'85

Next dividend meeting: Oct. 29'85.

Capitalization

Long Term Debt: $5,805,000,000.

Cum. Red. Preferred Stock: $129,000,000.

Cum. Red. Preference Stock: $597,000,000.

Common Stock: 147,578,133 shs. ($5 par).
Institutions hold about 47%.
Shareholders of record: 211,689.

Office—Tenneco Building, (P.O. Box 2511), Houston, Texas 77002. **Tel**—(713) 757-3907. **Chrmn & CEO**—J. L. Ketelsen. **Pres**—J. P. Diesel. **SVP-Secy**—W. W. Sapp. **Treas**—R. A. Robinson. **Investor Contact**—T. Tyler. **Dirs**—W. M. Blumenthal, J. P. Diesel, P. T. Flawn, J. B. Foster, H. U. Harris, Jr., B. K. Johnson, J. L. Ketelsen, B. J. Mackin, A. S. Plastow, K. W. Reese, J. J. Sisco. **Transfer Agent & Registrar**—Republic Bank Houston. **Incorporated** in Delaware in 1947.

 John J. Bilardello

Tenneco Inc.

2201

NYSE Symbol TGT Options on ASE (Feb-May-Aug-Nov) In S&P 500

Price	Range	P-E Ratio	Dividend	Yield	S&P Ranking
Sep. 30'85 37⅝	1985 45¼-36½	13	2.92	7.8%	A

Summary

This diversified company derives more than two-thirds of its profits from integrated oil and natural gas pipeline operations, with the balance from construction and farm equipment, shipbuilding, agriculture and land development, automotive components, packaging, and life insurance. The company has positioned itself to take advantage of any upturn in the energy industry. Profits in 1986 should benefit from greater gas throughput, reflecting the acquisition of pipelines from Goodyear.

Current Outlook

Share earnings for 1986 are expected to approximate $4.85, up from 1985's estimated $2.50, which is after a one-time charge of $1.65 for the write-offs of the Great Plains coal gasification and Cathedral Bluffs shale oil projects.

Dividends are likely to rise from the $0.73 quarterly level.

Pipeline profits in 1986 should report good gains, reflecting the acquisition of Louisiana natural gas businesses from Goodyear. Exploration and production will rise, but profits will be flat due to lower prices. Refining and marketing activities should continue advancing due to operating efficiencies. Shipbuilding is still benefiting from increased defense spending. Construction and farm equipment should break even, while other segments show modest income.

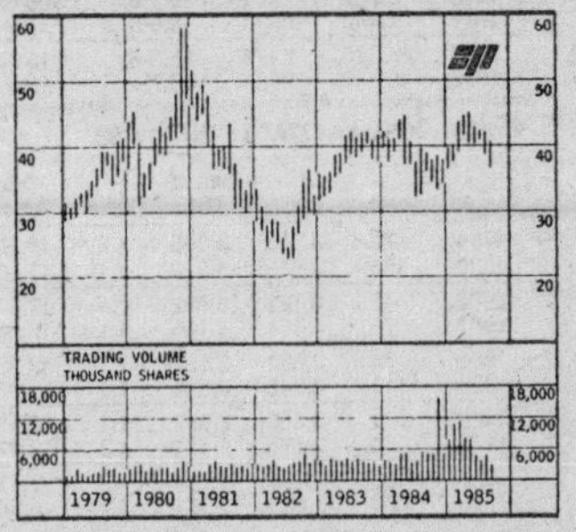

Operating Revenues (Billion $)

Quarter:	1985	1984	1983	1982
Mar.	3.72	3.88	3.61	3.77
Jun.	3.76	3.79	3.57	3.69
Sep.	---	3.38	3.43	3.63
Dec.	---	3.84	3.84	3.90
	---	14.89	14.45	14.98

Revenues for the six months ended June 30, 1985 declined 2.4%, year to year. Net income fell 39%. After preferred and preference dividends, share earnings were $1.37, versus $2.45.

Common Share Earnings ($)

Quarter:	1985	1984	1983	1982
Mar.	0.34	1.00	0.70	0.88
Jun.	1.03	1.46	1.38	1.66
Sep.	Ed0.50	0.76	1.04	1.40
Dec.	E1.63	0.80	1.63	1.96
	E2.50	4.01	4.75	5.90

Important Developments

Aug. '85—TGT wrote off substantially all of its investments in the Great Plains coal gasification project (in which it had a 30% stake) and the Cathedral Bluffs shale oil project (a 50% stake), resulting in an estimated one-time charge of $240 million or $1.65 a share against 1985 third quarter income. The cash impact will be about $35 million after the recapture of certain tax credits.

Jul. '85—TGT acquired certain natural gas businesses from the Goodyear Tire and Rubber Co. for cash and assumed debt totaling more than $500 million. The acquired companies, with 2,770 miles of pipelines, introduce TGT to the important Louisiana industrial market. Throughput of 1 bcf daily from the acquired pipelines will double Tenngasco's daily volumes.

Next earnings report due in late October.

Per Share Data ($)

Yr. End Dec. 31	1984	1983	1982	[1]1981	[1]1980	[1]1979	1978	[1]1977	1976	1975
Book Value	41.24	41.27	39.62	38.45	34.74	30.93	30.80	28.79	26.35	23.49
Earnings[3]	4.01	4.75	5.90	[2]6.01	[2]5.95	[2]5.30	[2]4.53	[2]4.38	[2]4.33	[2]4.15
Dividends	2.83	2.74	2.63	2.60	2.45	2.25	2.05	1.94	1.82	1.68
Payout Ratio	71%	58%	46%	45%	43%	44%	46%	45%	44%	43%
Prices—High	44¾	42⅜	36½	51⅞	58⅜	41½	34½	37¼	37⅜	27⅜
Low	32⅜	31⅞	22⅞	29⅞	31¼	29	28	28½	26	19¾
P/E Ratio—	11-8	9-7	6-4	9-5	10-5	8-5	8-6	9-7	9-6	7-5

Data as orig. reptd. 1. Reflects merger or acquisition. 2. Ful. dil.: 5.99 in 1981, 5.94 in 1980, 5.16 in 1979, 4.30 in 1978, 4.11 in 1977, 3.92 in 1976, 3.63 in 1975. 3. Bef. results of disc. opers. of -0.16 in 1982. d-Deficit. E-Estimated.

Standard NYSE Stock Reports
Vol. 52/No. 193/Sec. 22

October 7, 1985

Standard & Poor's Corp.
25 Broadway, NY, NY 10004

business and still giving a reasonable dividend, but in 1982 it was keeping 54% and paying out more than ever. That's a very healthy condition.

However, investors come in a variety of temperaments. Some are easy come easy go; they are too casual and often wind up with their money gone. Some buy into IBM, and when it drops a point they call their financial advisor and want to know what on earth has happened! They are genuinely upset by the slightest downward movement. There's an enormous difference in people's ability to withstand or even to think about risk. It's a good idea to explore your own risk-taking tolerance and take it into consideration with any investment program. Presumably you want peace of mind. You want to be able to sleep without nightmares of losing everything you have, and if possible, you want to sustain or come close to the standard of living you had when your husband was alive.

To a person who gets upset when IBM drops a point ($1.00), I suggest she check back in three weeks. By then IBM will probably have given back her dollar. When people understand how little is involved, they sometimes become quite upset with themselves. Often people don't understand how small an amount of money they are nervous about. They simply see a minus next to the number in the price column and start to panic. There are also the ones who are too careless; they want a stock because it appeals to them for some reason, regardless of any logic or what they have to pay for it. That's like betting on a racehorse because you like the color of its shiny coat. Basically, you have to know yourself, to know what kind of emotional fortitude you have, and then buy the kind of stocks you feel comfortable with.

To illustrate, we'll look at Applied Materials, the second company in the portfolio. Applied Materials is not listed on either exchange; it trades over-the-counter. In order to be listed on the New York or American Stock Exchanges, a company has to be of a certain size, have a certain number of sales, and a certain number of stockholders. However, some companies that could meet those standards choose to remain unlisted. Applied Materials at the time of writing was quoted 30 bid and 30¼ asked; the price range per share of the stock in 1982 and 1983 was between 22¼ and 48¾; and it paid no dividend so there was no yield. "Bid" means that someone was willing to pay $30 for a share of the stock, and "asked" means the owner was willing to sell at 30¼.

Standard & Poor's gives Applied Materials, an independent producer of wafer fabrication systems for increasing productivity in the semi-conductor industry, a C rating. Obviously, this is a rather new field. The earnings went from $1.06 to $1.37, then $.40 and $1.90, and then they dropped back to $.32 for the next 12 months. So no dividend—one point worth noticing. This is a company in an evolving industry; everything rides on its financial success and the acceptance of its products. Tenneco gives a 7% return, and with Applied Materials there is none at all. You don't even know if this company will be in business another year. On the other hand, it could be on the cutting edge of its particular technology.

Why then would anybody buy it? People buy this stock because they think wafer fabrications systems are the coming thing in this computer age. The company might turn out to be another Xerox which in decades past multiplied the value of the early investor's shares in a legendary fashion. They recognize they are taking a risk, and getting no dividend. You would only buy this stock if you felt you had money to burn. A father told his daughter as she was setting off for a weekend in Reno "Don't bet any more money than you can afford to throw into the Truckee River." That is equally true here. This is for gambling money, not must-have-for-income money.

Your money should have a purpose tag affixed to it, or parts of it. "This amount is what I absolutely must have to live on"; "This is for my barge trip in France." You buy stocks to do certain specific things for you. Your plans may not always work out, but you haven't a chance of success if you don't know what you are trying to accomplish in the first place.

Depending on what is happening to the stock market, some years a P/E of 9 has been the bottom P/E and some years 6 has been the top; try to find the average. If you bought a stock for 11 times earnings, what would be your relative chances of it going up or down? If the historical mean has been 8, and you buy for higher than that, the odds are that it is likely to go down rather than up. That is why studying the historical P/E ratio is so important.

Sometimes things happen that change the ratio. For example, an internal development might take place such as the board chairman dropping dead on the golf course. An external event can affect the P/E, too, such as when the Defense Department cancels a contract and the stock price is affected by it. This sort of thing happened to Caterpillar Tractor after the Soviets got heavy-handed in Poland and President Reagan decided that no American company should participate in the construction of the proposed natural gas pipeline from the Soviet Union to Western Europe—Caterpillar had sizeable contracts for a share of the pipeline construction. The stock suffered dramatically as you saw.

Ultimately, the most important thing about a company is the hardest thing to find out about—what kind of judgment it has. That really tells the tale, but the only way one can judge it or guess how a company will do in the future is by taking a look at how it has done in the past. And, of course, watch for current news. An announcement about a new president for a company can be very important because this can change the company's whole pattern. The head of a company can make a material difference.

Investors are something like race track bettors. Some put their money down at the $2 cage and say, "I want to bet on the horse with the spots." Others won't put down a dime until they know the horse's bloodlines, its trainer, the state of the track, and the owners. It's very much the same with stocks. As I've said, you have to know what you are doing and what you want. You have to know if you want something conservative and steady that has a good chance for a rising income over the next ten years. Traders, people who buy and sell their stocks a lot trying to take a profit, often come out of a ten-year span with zero benefit. Taxes and commissions, which have to be paid every time a stock is bought or sold, and mistakes averaged with successes can come out even. Investors who think a lot first, do research, buy, and for the most part hold, generally do better if they have shown good sense.

One broker says it is better to sell, if you are selling, on the way *down* from a stock price of 50 than on the way up to 50. For example, if you have a stock with a P/E ratio of 9 and one day you look in the paper and see that it has moved up to 15 times earnings, that would be time to give your stock a second thought. You might decide the valuation of this stock is a little high, that never before had it sold at 15 times earnings, so you get uneasy and decide to get out. The most you can hope for is to be right two-thirds of the time. If you hit a lemon, don't try to make lemonade of it—sell it. Any year, and any day of the year, a lot of stocks sell for more than they are worth and lots sell for less.

As to bonds, at this time of writing, bond holders are suffering if they want to sell because as interest rates went up, the value of their bonds went down—and down. They pray the Fed will loosen up its tight money policy a bit, and the administration will constrain the budget deficit sufficiently that interest rates will come down. Then the capital value of their bonds will go up.

If a good stock you own is coming down in price, and you notice that the P/E has dropped from 15 to 7 times earnings, that the earnings and dividends continue to rise, and the management hasn't been fired, it may be a good time to buy some more.

Sylvia Porter tells how P/Es can help you spot bargains in the stock market. "Many analysts and experienced investors use P/E ratios, that is the current price divided by the earnings per share of a stock, to find undervalued situations in which they might want to invest.

"If a stock has historically never had a P/E ratio lower than 5, and its earnings seem headed up, you would seem to be taking little risk in buying when its P/E ratio was 5. The likelihood that the stock will go down further seems fairly slim. On the other hand, the potential upward movement of the stock seems promising."

The earnings per share movement is documented in the Standard & Poor's stock report sheets and also in their *Stock Guide*.

"Now take the reverse situation," she says. "You are looking at a company that has never had a P/E lower than 5 or higher than 18. If you buy that stock when its P/E ratio is at its high point, 18, you are obviously taking a bigger risk, for the likelihood that it will go up depends almost entirely on a sharp increase in its future earnings."

A word should be said about the takeovers that have been so numerous in recent years and generally very popular among the shareholders of the company being taken over because the price of that stock usually starts to climb. When the negotiations are over, the price paid for the shares of the company is often considerably above where it stood at the time the word got out, so the shareholders will reap a handsome profit.

An example was the R.J. Reynolds Industries, Inc., offer to buy Heublein, Inc., for nearly $1.56 billion. R.J. Reynolds, first known as the maker of Camel cigarettes, is still in domestic and international tobaccos, but it also owns Del Monte Corp., the largest canner of fruits and vegetables. Heublein, besides its spirits group, which included Smirnoff Vodka, Harvey's Bristol Cream Sherry, Don Z Rum, Jose Cuevo Tequila and a couple of wineries, also owned Kentucky Fried Chicken, A.1. Steak Sauce, Ortega Mexican Food, and a popular mustard.

Though I have no insight into the corporate thinking involved, it is possible that Reynolds decided to expand its holdings in the food and spirits area and came to the conclusion that it would be a lot simpler and cheaper to buy a going company with good products and a healthy balance sheet than to venture into the field from scratch with heavy start up and promotional costs. In a ten-day period starting before there was even a good rumor that Reynolds was interested in Heublein (another company had been making overtures to it which were rejected), the stock went from 43 to 57.

In such situations, an oil company may buy an office systems company, a food company may buy a publishing house. Annual reports give an interesting inventory of who owns what. The purpose for the buying company is usually diversification. Not long ago an oil company offered to buy a copper company for a price that was almost twice the price of the copper company's stock. But the copper company refused, saying the value of what they had in the ground in assets indicated that the oil company's offer was too low.

Often, during a controversy like this, the New York Stock Exchange stops trading in the stock. This time they didn't and during the controversy the stock of the copper company went up 27 points in one day.

If you find yourself in a bidding war, that is, owning a stock whose company is being looked at as a possible takeover, it can be very exciting. If you have never read the financial pages before, you will start to if a company you are in is the object of a bidding war because you are potentially making so much money. You watch the situation develop and try to figure out who is going to win (if several competing companies are involved) and where the most money is. Usually, you will come out smelling like a rose, maybe not the biggest rose but a good sized one.

Though mutual funds were already discussed generally in previous chapters, I want to say a few more words about them that may be useful. Mutual funds are nothing more nor less than a portfolio, or a mix, of investments in sizeable quantities. Mutual funds are required by law to state in their brochures exactly what they are trying to do, what their goals and objectives are. One, called the Union Income Fund, states, "The fund's objectives are to produce high current income with what is believed to be prudent risk of capital and the possibility of improved income and capital over the longer term."

You can read quite a few of these stated goals and check out the last years' performance of those that sound interesting to you. Then write for their information and take a look at what they own. Such information is not boilerplate. It should be taken very literally, and if you don't agree with what the fund is trying to do or are uncomfortable with it, don't get involved. Why support something you don't agree with?

Some investors are bothered by certain things that go on in our economy and by some of the things we make, such as nuclear weapons. While they may not go to the length of withholding part of their income taxes because they don't want to pay for such things, they still do not wish to support them nor invest their money in a company that makes them no matter how successful the company is nor how much money it would make for the investor. There are funds described by David Dietz, a syndicated financial writer, especially for this growing number of individual investors who feel there is more to investing than just the numbers. They feel it is nice to make money, but it's just as important to satisfy their consciences. For them, any investment must pass muster on social as well as financial grounds.

"The belief," says Stephen Moody, a portfolio manager with a Boston bank, "is that it must be possible to earn a reasonable return" without having to invest in something socially undesirable to the investor. He also says the relatively short history of guiding socially concerned investments at the United States Trust Company in Boston shows that returns are staying ahead of inflation, perhaps a key consideration. Depending on who is doing the investing, of course, what constitutes a "socially responsible" company can vary widely. "In broad terms," says Dietz, "such a company would not produce military equipment nor engage in defense contract work, does no business with regimes that violate human rights, does not engage in unfair labor practices, has no nuclear power interest, and has avoided practices that might be judged harmful to the environment."

There are several such funds. The Dreyfus Third Century Fund in New York is one. Pax World Fund in Portsmouth, New Hampshire, is another. In Boston, Foursquare will not invest in alcoholic beverages, tobacco, or drug concerns. Research on such corporate policy is conducted by the Council on Economic Priorities in New York and the Northern

California Interfaith Committee on Corporate Responsibility headquartered in San Francisco.

After all this discussion of putting money to work in different ways, perhaps you are ready to move out on your own in whichever channel seems suited to your needs and the amount of money you have to invest. It is not the purpose of the book to encourage you to make major financial decisions without good professional guidance. The exception is selecting among the various mutual funds where the research available will be as clear to you as to anyone else. Nor do I promote any of the investments used as illustrations—things change over time. I have dealt with the past. You are looking toward the future. My purpose is to interest you sufficiently in what someone else may be doing on your behalf so that eventually you will become very knowledgeable about every bond and stock certificate that rests in your safe deposit box. Most of all, you will have confidence in where you stand now and can approach future decisions with the equanimity that comes with understanding.

The next chapter deals, among other things, with drawing up your own net worth statement.

CHAPTER NINE

Your Financial and Personal Net Worth

One more financial exercise you should perform as you prepare to get a firm grip on your finances is the preparation of your own net worth statement. You've seen one from a company, Merck, and you know that the only requirement is to add up what you own, and subtract from that what you owe. The result is what you are worth when you go to bed tonight. You may be worth more or less by tomorrow night, depending on what happens in the financial markets tomorrow.

If, for instance, Congress should decide to make annual reductions instead of increases in appropriations, across the board, the decline in the national budget would be significant: interest rates would start to tumble, there might be money to lend for housing at rates people could afford, the interest on the national debt would shrink, employment would go up and unemployment down, more tax revenue would flow into the Treasury, and we might even return to an era that now seems as though it never was, when financial stability was taken for granted and a 6% return on a bond seemed a very solid investment.

Stretch your imagination to contemplate the economic results of shifting massive expenditures from preparations for war to the more prosaic problems of world hunger, high birthrates, insufficient water supplies, infant mortality, and the staggering problem in this country of employment for millions so undereducated and ill-equipped there seems no room for them in an age when robots build automobiles and transportation systems are run by computers.

Some adjustments could be devastating, among them our balance of trade figures, because so many of the goods we sell abroad are armaments, high-tech weapons. However pleasant the prospect might be of adapting to an economy and a government more concerned with repairing the crumbling interstate highway system than digging invisible holes in the ground to store MX missiles, it would not be painless.

Consider that when World War II ended in 1945, there was widespread fear of a return to the Depression. In *The Glory and the Dream,* William Manchester records that we were warned to prepare for hungry veterans roaming the streets in packs. "Some economists foresaw another 1932 . . . political scientists warned of revolution. The harder they looked, the more convinced employers were that there was no way to turn industry's juggernaut of superproductivity toward peaceful pursuits without stumbling into disaster."

Hindsight renders such gloom unbelievable, considering the unprecedented prosperity that followed, but at the time it was real enough.

Then, as now, individuals established their own objectives, and tried to make plans to achieve them. No one but you can set your goals. That is the important thing to bear in mind.

The Net Worth Statement sample on page 147 is a simple

listing of the elements involved. When that is completed, perhaps it will help you realize that as a matter of fact you are running a small business from which you hope to make a profit.

As Louis Rukeyser says, "Wall Street provides merchandise for shoppers with vastly different financial needs and desires. Some will be looking for long-term growth—for that quality stock with a unique product or service that in each new business cycle ends up in earnings and price a little higher than before. It is a course that takes initial care, continual attention and permanent patience, but it has been a consistent winner for millions. Others define their goals differently; they may, for example, require a more immediate return on their securities or wish to test their speculative agility. The important thing is that neither these nor other aspirations have any exclusive claim to legitimacy or probability of success—but that the investor's goals must in some way be defined before he begins."

Your own progress in planning your future will come at a faster pace once the uncertainties about your finances clear away. When you know where you stand, you are free to make the personal decisions about the sort of life you want to live. Probably the choices are more varied than you thought. Are there avenues from your past you never were able to follow? A lot of women retrieve former interests they were not able to pursue fully and go back to school to develop them further. Should you try that, probably a happy surprise is in store. If you find yourself in a class with most of the students half your age or less, you will probably discover that simply in the process of living more years than they have, you have picked up skills and knowledge that makes college level work a lot easier now than it was the first time around.

Maybe you prefer the discipline of a job, for love or money, which is good therapy and automatically introduces

Net Worth Statement

of

as of

Assets

Cash

Checking account(s) ______

Savings account(s) ______

Money Market fund(s) ______

Total ______

*Investments**

Stocks ______

Bonds ______

Real property ______

Personal property ______

CDs ______

T-bills ______

Art works ______

Other collectibles ______

Other investments ______

Total ______

Other Assets

Loans due me ______

Trust participation ______

Business participation ______

Other ______

Total ______

Total Assets ______

Liabilities

Obligations due

Rent ______

Utilities ______

Taxes—income & property ______

Insurance premiums—auto, life, homeowners ______

Credit cards—Visa, Master Charge, etc. ______

Total ______

Other obligations

Installment balances due ______

Real estate loan balances due ______

Home mortgage balance due ______

Other loan balances due ______

Total ______

Total Liabilities ______

Subtract Liabilities from Assets

Assets ______

Liabilities ______

My Net Worth is ______

*Indicate Cost (C) or Market Value (MV) for each category

you to a new set of people and demands that lift you out of yourself. For a paid job, career counseling is available at almost any educational center, some especially directed toward women like yourself. If you aren't sure about what skills you have beyond the ones you have developed and prefer a change from, seek out a reputable vocational guidance center that offers a battery of tests. Some tests take a week to complete. When you have finished them you already feel like a new woman because your thinking ability has been challenged so much. When your test has been analyzed, you will be directed toward certain fields. Such centers rarely provide a placement service, too, but they may make suggestions.

Remember that while you have been away from the job market, a lot of legislation has been passed to protect you from discrimination in employment because of your sex or your age, so pursue any idea you have. It won't be any harder than that first visit you made to the lawyer's office by yourself.

If up to now your outside activities have been for the public good, not for pay, don't denigrate them as "just" volunteer work. They may have been excellent training for jobs pulling down a salary. When you have the time, it could give you a lot of satisfaction to work up a biographical sketch of yourself, or a resume, as they are called in the professional and business world. If you think back over your own past, you may be surprised at the amount of time and energy you have given away in the interest of others.

Should you now be in what are called the golden years, there is probably a senior citizen counseling center in your community that can give you guidance about both paid and volunteer jobs. It's nothing to rush into but worth keeping in mind for the time, which will surely come, when you have mastered the financial planning and executing necessary to establish yourself as an independent woman in charge of her own life. And it's one with many options open to you."

On the matter of travel, though a "Love Boat" sort of cruise may not appeal to you, there are all sorts of other trips that can be fascinating. One such is a whale viewing cruise, in the company of others intrigued by the glorious mammals that converse in a complex language man has yet to understand. In a small rubber raft you can look over the side and see a whale sliding underneath the bottom perhaps six inches under your feet. If it sneezed, you would all go into the water. That rarely happens—the whale seems to understand that you mean it no harm, and he will probably breach up through the water near you, and fix the boatload with his small, sharp eye until his massive head slips down beneath the surface.

Travel agents probably have information about such specialized expeditions, natural history trips, tours specializing in various minerals and gems, archeological explorations of all kinds. One outfit that started small and has greatly expanded its scope in recent years is "Biological Journeys," 1876 Ocean Avenue, McKinleyville, CA 95521.

Of one thing you can be sure, the people you will meet on such a trip are going to be interesting because they share a focus, and you will also be impressed with the vast amount of information the tour leaders have amassed about the flora and fauna of out-of-the-way parts of the globe.

Fishing, birdwatching, wild flowers, the infinity of life in the marshlands, all have organizations devoted to the pursuit of knowledge in their specialized fields. Rock hounds, for instance, have exhibits and conventions periodically in various parts of the country, and local clubs all over.

Perhaps none of these outdoor distractions appeals to you. There are bridge and book clubs everywhere, language classes, computer classes, groups devoted to music, classes in every sort of art form including quilting, which seems to have revived people's interest and is a sociable sort of activity.

Once you decide you want to climb out of your shell and start asking questions about what is available, you will begin to get answers in profusion. All it takes is a little initiative on your part.

As you start to feel better, more confident and physically stronger, it will come to you that despite your sense of loss and in place of what you had, you now are a free woman; free that is, to pursue a sort of living pattern never before possible since you need not be concerned about the welfare and preferences of anyone else. You can suit yourself, perhaps for the first time in your life.

However, before you set off on a personal odyssey of self-fulfillment, there are a couple of items to take care of. The first is your new will. This should include estate planning in depth to find the best way or ways of reducing the tax consequences to your heirs of whatever they will inherit from you. Naturally, this process involves a lawyer. Tax laws are changing so rapidly, there may be new avenues open that did not exist a few years ago.

Then there is the matter of how much you want your children, if you have any, to know about your personal affairs. If the relationship between you is open, I believe it would give you a sense of having tidied things up to consult them before you make your will, possibly after talking it over first with the lawyer, who will have ideas regarding the age at which it may be wise to let them have their share outright.

You would also want to select several possibilities as executor, all of them a good deal younger than you so the prospect of one of the choices being around to handle the matter are reasonably good.

It is my personal belief that the more your heirs know about your finances, assuming they are responsible people, the more openly you can discuss the future with them. In all probability, they will urge you to spend freely on yourself during your lifetime, not realizing that a great impediment to such indulgence is the fact that you have no idea of your own terminal date and would not like to arrive at your 104th birthday with only 10 shares of IBM left to support you. That uncertainty has no doubt benefitted the children of many parents who would otherwise happily have squandered away what they had.

Another procedure that contributes to a sense of order in your life is to make an inventory of what you have—not just stocks and bonds, but personal possessions, especially if they have a value or a history that your heirs may be ignorant of. You may have an autographed first edition of a book by a writer who has become valued over the years, or a Chinese antique that doesn't look like much but is quite valuable. Such ignorance among heirs is the source of the treasures one hears about picked up at flea markets for a pittance—a Chinese T'ang warrior for $9, for instance.

And finally, if you have grandchildren, by the time they are in their forties they will be very interested in the sort of life you led, especially in your early days, which will seem totally unreal to them. Consider telling them or writing it all out. To them the era in which you grew up seems more distant than the moon. Imagine growing up without television, only one telephone in the house on which you gave a number to an operator, an icebox that was supplied by the iceman who carted in a huge block of ice every other day, no supermarkets, soundless black and white movies, no convenience foods, large family gatherings on Sundays—whatever the components of your early days and the lives of your parents, especially what you did for entertainment. One day, they will find such a family history not only of great interest but of support, finally grasping something of their roots.

You might also find another man with whom you want to share a part or all of your life. If you are so fortunate, you should consider adopting for yourself the mores of the young that took you so long to accept in the beginning. Take a trip with him, have him come stay with you for a while, get to know far more about him than you probably knew about your husband before you married him.

Hotels, motels, ships, and travel agents no longer evince the slightest surprise at reservations made for a double accommodations in the names of Mr. John Smith and Mrs. Shirley Evans, nor will the people you meet on such excursions. They may be interested, but they won't be shocked.

Delay, even though you know the time ahead is not endless, is only sensible because neither of you is probably going to want to change the habits acquired over years or even be able to, if you wanted. Neither of you is as adaptable as you were, and there is always the matter of your estates. Again, the attorney can be a big help in anticipating complications, explaining the various ways such things can be handled.

Should you remarry, it could be a wonderful thing for you but consider postponing such a decision until you have become quite accustomed to handling your own affairs and have things worked out to the point that they are no longer a constant preoccupation.

Short of remarriage, as your social life has revived and you no longer hesitate to have people for dinner because there is no host, you may find old friends from years ago, or friends of your husband, who are now single men. All sorts of possibilities can develop if you are willing and able to dispense with the moral prohibitions that surrounded you when you were a single woman years ago.

Today, there is nothing wrong with calling a man up and inviting him to go out to dinner with you, sharing the check or as your guest—or the opera, the movies, a motor trip, a visit to Hawaii or Bermuda, or whatever. Your friends will be delighted, and you will feel more like a whole person. There is no reason to confine your companionship to only one man if several have different attractions that interest you. If you have come to cherish your independence now, it need not confine you to a solitary existence.

Though you may not feel entirely a part of the era of the liberated woman, the fact remains that you *are* one. You are living a new life, yours to design as you wish. Though you have lost the luxury of having someone else assume the final responsibility for your financial well-being, you have gained a new maturity through the acquisition of some relatively sophisticated understanding of what goes on in the money world. Your sense of security must be a lot stronger, for you are now a woman competent to deal with her world.

You've done well on a long hard road. Congratulations and good luck!